About the Author

Derek Pedley joined *The West Australian* in Perth as a cadet journalist in 1990 and is now a news sub editor at *The Advertiser* in Adelaide.

He has reported on Brenden Abbott's crimes since 1994 and travelled to eight cities in the course of researching this book.

The hunt for
Brenden James Abbott

no fixed address

by Derek Pedley

HarperCollinsPublishers

Permission to use the images that appear on the cover of this book
was kindly granted by the following:

Western Australia Police Service: semi-automatic weapon (top left);
prison window with missing steel bars (used on back cover and bottom middle
of front cover); gun, with accessories (bottom right);
WA Police forensic ruler (bottom and top).
South Australia Police Service: bandits robbing bank, Adelaide, 1991 (main cover shot).
Queensland Police Service: photoboard of the possible appearance variations of
Brenden James Abbott (ghosted back).
NT News: Guns, cash etc. seized from Abbott in Darwin, 1998 (bottom left).

HarperCollins*Publishers*

First published in Australia in 1999
by HarperCollins*Publishers* Pty Limited
ACN 009 913 517
A member of the HarperCollins*Publishers* (Australia) Pty Limited Group
http://www.harpercollins.com.au

Copyright © Derek Pedley 1999

HarperCollins*Publishers*
25 Ryde Road, Pymble, Sydney, NSW 2073, Australia
31 View Road, Glenfield, Auckland 10, New Zealand
77-85 Fulham Palace Road, London W6 8JB, United Kingdom
Hazelton Lanes, 55 Avenue Road, Suite 2900, Toronto, Ontario M5R 3L2
and 1995 Markham Road, Scarborough, Ontario M1B 5M8, Canada
10 East 53rd Street, New York NY 10022, USA

National Library of Australia Cataloguing-in-Publication data:

Pedley, Derek, 1972- .
No fixed address: the hunt for Brenden James Abbott.
ISBN 0 7322 6664 5.
1. Abbott, Brenden James. 2. Criminals - Australia.
3. Violent crimes - Australia. I. Title.
364.1552092

Printed in Australia by Griffin Press Pty Ltd Adelaide.

6 5 4 3 2 1   99 00 01 02

Acknowledgments

My sincere thanks to the dozens of police officers across Australia who made this book possible, particularly Detectives Sid Thomas, Glen Potter, Jeff Beaman, Glen Prichard, Jack Lee and Rob King.

Many newspapers and journalists gave freely of their time and knowledge, particularly the *Courier-Mail* and the paper's chief police reporter, Paula Doneman, *The West Australian* and the *NT News*, and NT Police Media Director Jane Munday.

Advertiser Editor Steve Howard, Night Editor Mike Jaensch and News Editor Mark Robinson provided endless support, patience and humour.

Special thanks to Paul Murray and Luke Morfesse at *The West Australian*, who showed faith through trying times, and Michael Ioannakis, a mate when it mattered.

My love and deep gratitude to my parents, John and Phyllis Pedley, for their constant support, and Belinda, who was there through it all and always believed.

Contents

The hunt for
Brenden James Abbott

Chapter 1

The Belmont job

'Everybody down. We want the money. We don't want to hurt anybody and we don't want no fuckin' heroes pushing buttons.'

— Brenden Abbott to bank staff,
Perth, 29 May 1987

Crouched in the darkness of the bank ceiling, Brenden Abbott allowed himself a smile as he watched the staff prepare for opening. He checked his watch: 8.40 am, Friday. Almost time.

Would it work? He ran through the checklist.

Weapons? Shotgun and .45s. *Check.*

Disguises? Overalls, balaclavas and gloves. *Check.*

Entry point through ceiling? Identified during surveillance. *Check.*

Number of staff, usual habits, location of vault, time required? As above. *Check.*

Getaway car, route, hotel arrangements? In place, planned and arranged. *Check.*

Intelligence on police locations, movements, reaction time? Programmed scanner. *Check.*

In his mind, there was every reason for Peter Lievense to take a chance. Out of work for five months. No money. No bloody food in the house. It didn't surprise him. Life, in general, hadn't been kind to the 26-year-old, later described as a 'softly spoken country boy' by his lawyer. Parents divorced at age four. A ten-year ride on the foster home merry-go-round. Six different schools. Unskilled. Unemployed. Not a pretty picture. So when his old mate Brenden Abbott came knocking on the night of Thursday, 28 May 1987, he thought his luck was about to change.

Even then, Abbott had a criminal reputation — although it extended only as far as Perth's eastern suburbs and the office of the Criminal Investigation Branch (CIB) Break Squad. He had perfected the art of electrical store burglaries and there was money to be made helping him shift the gear. But on this particular night, Abbott had something bigger in mind.

Lievense and his girlfriend were watching TV when Abbott and another of his mates, David Stabback, arrived. 'Let's go in the kitchen. There's something we need to talk about,' Abbott said, eyeing Lievense's girlfriend in the lounge room.

They settled down at the kitchen table and got straight down to business.

'We're going to break into a bank and stick it up in the morning while the staff are there, after the time locks open the safe. We need a driver, and some tools,' Abbott said.

'Which bank?' Lievense asked.

Abbott laughed. 'That's the one, mate. Which Bank. Just drop us off at the bank tonight, then pick us up from the hotel down the road in the morning.'

Driving a car ... no rough stuff, no risks. And a couple of grand to keep the wolves from the door. He didn't hesitate. 'I'm in.'

But there was no rush. The Belmont Hotel, across the road from the Commonwealth Bank branch Abbott had selected, was still open. Better to wait until after closing time. Give the drunks a chance to hit the road. So they settled in for an evening of TV and left about midnight.

Lievense was back on the lounge within minutes, having left Abbott and Stabback huddled in shadows near the bank. They checked the area and then crept onto the roof with tools borrowed from Lievense. Working quickly, they cut a discreet hole in the corrugated roof, folded it back and squeezed through. This was the crucial moment. Would the alarm activate? Abbott wasn't taking any chances. Carrying a scanner with police frequencies was already standard operating procedure for the 25-year-old. If the silent alarm was triggered, he wanted to know about it before the local divisional van came tearing down the street. But the night remained still.

was asleep on the couch — it was around 3 am — when Abbott walked in and shook him awake. 'In the morning I'll come past and toot the horn. Come to the hotel and pick me up,' he told him.

Lievense, still half asleep, mumbled his agreement. 'Yeah, whatever mate.' He went back to sleep and Abbott and Stabback left, probably in the getaway car stolen earlier that night.

Abbott, a car enthusiast of some note, had selected a new Mitsubishi Cordia turbo from a car yard in a nearby suburb. They left it in the bank's parking area, then climbed back into the ceiling to begin the tense wait for daylight.

This would be no beginner's operation. Armed Robbery Squad detectives who later pieced it together recognised the signs of men confident in their work. Apart from the last-minute recruitment of Lievense and his tools, it was planned to the last detail. And it was startlingly similar to a job on the nearby Rural and Industries (R&I) Bank branch only weeks before. An armed man had entered the bank while another waited outside in a stolen Mitsubishi Cordia. A security camera recorded a picture of a single eye peering through a balaclava just before it was sprayed with paint and the bank was robbed. 'It was him,' says one detective who pursued Abbott. 'I'll never forget his eyes. Ice cold.'

There were other jobs, too. But getting enough evidence for an armed robbery arrest warrant requires a great deal more than suspicion. Physical evidence, positive identifications, confessions. Without at least one of these elements, a detective seeking a conviction labours in vain.

But Abbott left nothing and gave nothing away. He made his mistakes, but he was becoming the proverbial boy scout — always prepared. The guns had come from Stabback, another young villain who had already served a stretch for armed robbery. About a week earlier, he drove a stolen panel van through the window of WA Guns and Ammo in south-east suburban Maddington, and grabbed 21 handguns — ten grand's worth — from a display case. Abbott liked choice. And he liked quality equipment. As Lievense would later say: 'Brenden always carries a handgun in a holster on his shoulder. He's always got it with him. It's a .45 pistol magazine job.'

As the bank staff began trickling in at about 8.20 that morning, Abbott felt confident he had covered all the bases. The timing of their entry into the office was the key. Go too soon, before all the staff have arrived, and risk being interrupted. Or worse, face an agonising wait for the safe lock to release. Wait too long, and the duress alarms and cameras would be switched on and the front door would be open.

Karl Langdon, bank teller and promising young Subiaco footballer, arrived for work at about 8.20. An impressive white sports car was parked in his usual spot. He couldn't resist an admiring glance as he passed. By 8.45, he and his colleagues were settled at their desks, preparing for the day ahead.

Suddenly, a thundering crash from the ceiling broke the silence. It was a sound which came to be feared by bank staff around the nation over the next 11 years. Abbott dived through the ceiling first, springing to his feet and waving a .45 pistol at the staff while Stabback, according to one of the witnesses, passed down the shotgun. One staff member was confused. She saw the overalls and thought the men were electricians who'd

'I was terrified,' the assistant manager said later. 'They were obviously trying to scare the living daylights out of us — which they did, of course. I said: "Please don't shoot me, mate. There's plenty of money in there".'

Abbott controlled the main banking chamber while Stabback took care of business. 'Get the fucking cash out,' Stabback told the assistant manager in the vault. Easier said than done.

'Listen, mate. I can't get it out. I need [another employee's] combination,' he pleaded.

'Well fucking get them, then.'

The other employee — the woman who had mistaken the pair for electricians — was quick to assist, eager to get rid of the foul-mouthed thugs. But her colleague was struggling to keep a grip. 'Please concentrate very hard, because I don't think I'll be able to get it [the combination] off. My hand's shaking too much,' he told her.

Under a barrage of threats and abuse, the safe and several compartments within were eventually opened. The two bank employees removed the money tins, but Stabback's bag was too small. The woman struggled to push it all in.

'Hurry up, you fucking bitch.'

'Shut your guts,' she told him. What more did this guy want? Angry, she gave one of the tins a final shove, knocking Stabback off balance and off guard.

He pulled the trigger — accidentally, he later claimed — and the shot thundered like a cannon in the tiny vault. The bullet should have bounced around until it struck flesh. Instead, a wad of $5 notes was mortally wounded. Abbott, less than impressed, burst in. 'Dave, what the fuck are you doing? The cops are around the corner, let's go.' He should have known better. Using a real name during the commission of an armed robbery was beginner's stuff. And it was a handy break for the detectives who would later interview the bank staff.

'OK, but I'm not fuckin' going until I get that green tin,' Stabback replied. Good call. The tin contained $40 000 to $50 000 in notes, plus coins. All up, $112 730. A good day's work. Stabback grabbed the bag and, after a final warning to the staff, they bolted out the front door. A few seconds later Karl Langdon peered outside. The white sports car was disappearing into the distance.

A racing motor and car horn jolted Peter Lievense awake on the lounge. 'Christ, it's Brenden. He's really done it,' he thought. No sense in keeping the man waiting.

He drove to the Travelodge on the Great Eastern Highway, where Abbott had booked a room under one of his many aliases and was already opening the money tins. Stabback wanted to get moving, so Lievense took him back to his house to pick up his car and meet them later. Lievense then returned to the Travelodge, where Abbott was also keen to get out of the area.

to The Raffles, a hotel on the Swan River across town in Applecross. Abbott booked another room, and Stabback arrived soon after. The trio sat down to count the takings and soon came up with the bottom line — a job well done. Lievense grabbed a couple of grand. 'I'll get some more later. Don't want the missus finding out,' he told them. Stabback and Abbott split the rest. Now it was time to part ways.

Stabback went his own way while Lievense and Abbott drove to the Garratt Road Bridge to dispatch some of the guns left over from the ram raid on the Maddington gun shop. It was now mid-afternoon. Business over, it was time to enjoy the moment. Abbott waited in Lievense's vehicle while he went to a car hire firm on the Great Eastern Highway, Rivervale. 'Get me something flash, like a red Porsche,' Abbott told him. He settled for a black BMW and they parted ways.

The following Sunday, they enjoyed an afternoon of horse riding at Yanchep, north of Perth, celebrating their success on what would be their last day as friends. Later, Lievense drove Abbott to Tame Street, Dianella, where he paid cash for a Toyota LandCruiser. It was time to put the show back on the road.

Abbott's parole had been cancelled that month, although he had effectively been on the run since the previous December. Nollamara CIB had wanted a quiet chat about some electrical stores. Abbott wasn't feeling talkative. He slipped out the back door when the detective watching him was distracted. Since then, he had kept on the move with a stint in the north-west of the state, and frequent travels in the eastern states. Now it was time to widen his horizons further. He liked the laid-back atmosphere of the tropics, the wide open spaces, the anonymity of the outback. Darwin seemed like a good place to plan his next move.

Over at the Commonwealth Bank, the Armed Robbery Squad had spent the day of the robbery examining Abbott's handiwork. All they had was a name — Dave — a roomful of distraught victims and an empty vault.

So what led them to suspect Abbott? Even now, they aren't saying. Certainly he was known to them, but it seems there was little in the way of clues at the bank that could be considered a lead. And the Cordia wasn't found for several days.

There was only one conclusion — someone had talked. Even Abbott knew it. 'Who dobbed me in?' he asked the detectives after his arrest. Whoever it was had good information.

Within days, the detectives knew who was involved and immediately targeted the weak link — Lievense. His house on Armadale Road, Rivervale, was raided on June 3 and a red carrier bag containing $2354 was seized. He was an easy mark for detectives looking for a prosecution witness. The choice he faced was simple: 'Help catch Abbott and give evidence at his trial. The Director of Public Prosecutions [DPP] will have a word to the beak and you'll probably get a couple of years. Don't want to talk? Then get used to small rooms. Fremantle Prison has long-term vacancies.' It wasn't as appealing as the proposition Abbott had posed several days before. But Lievense wasn't doing a long stretch just for a couple of grand — he didn't care who Brenden Abbott was.

For the Armed Robbery Squad, it was a handy result — Stabback was quickly scooped up and Lievense was making the best of a bad situation. Now there was only the small matter of the third arrest.

Abbott was busy playing Jack Kerouac, Australian-style. He and another associate were heading north, unaware of the developments back in Perth. Travelling in Abbott's newly acquired four-wheel drive, they stopped for a break in Port Hedland, 1700 kilometres north of Perth.

Abbott was no stranger to the north-west town and the appropriately named Walkabout Inn where they stayed. He had worked as the assistant bar manager of the pub, after a mate gave him a job there a couple of years before. He had friends there and it was an obvious port of call for him. And for the police. So when Abbott made some calls back to Perth on June 4 and learned of the arrests of Lievense and Stabback, he left immediately.

They didn't miss him by much. Local detectives raided the hotel but found only his unfortunate mate. No matter — there are only so many ways out of country towns in the huge expanse of Western Australia's north: a couple of roads, easily monitored. And the airport.

Meanwhile, three detectives with the Armed Robbery Squad in Perth were puzzling over their options and how to cover them. Darwin detectives were fully briefed. Abbott wouldn't be leaving their airport without a set of handcuffs. But would he stick to his plan and head for the Northern Territory? They checked the airline schedules. Two flights due in to Perth Airport from the north-west.

Detective Sergeant Ian Brandis, in charge of the operation, wasn't taking any chances. But there was no time for briefings or complicated plans. Detectives Barry Lehmann and John Adams, the only other detectives in the office at the time, had to move quickly. They hastily assembled an arrest team of detectives and uniformed officers — borrowed from the Break Squad and the Hay Street Mall — and raced to the domestic terminal. Lehmann — who knew Abbott from his days at Nollamara CIB — was the best man to make the ID. He would wait on the tarmac with a uniformed officer (wearing a jacket) and make the ID if Abbott stepped from the plane. The rest of the troops would remain discreetly hidden near the baggage handlers' entrance, ready to pounce at Lehmann's signal. 'This could be ugly,' he thought. 'A bank robber, possibly armed, shielded by other passengers. Shoot-out, hostage situation. Front page headlines.'

He pushed the thoughts from his mind as the first flight landed. The passengers shuffled to the terminal. Nothing. Twenty minutes later, Flight 347 from Port Hedland taxied in. And there he was, the true picture of a hunted man, lagging behind the other passengers and reaching into his leather jacket as he scanned the area nervously.

'Oh Christ,' thought Lehmann. 'He's ready to go. This is full-on.'

'We don't want to alarm him,' he told the uniform. 'Stay back, I'll handle it.'

Abbott now increased his speed to catch up with the other passengers. Lehmann fell in behind, trying to keep up. And he was still acutely aware of Abbott's hand twitching inside his jacket.

Three metres. He drew his gun, pushed the other passengers aside and called out: 'Brenden Abbott! Freeze, police! On the ground now!'

Chapter 2

Starting out

'I think there is hope for Abbott . . . I would like him to have the opportunity of coming out as soon as possible.'
— Defence lawyer Ross Lonnie,
Perth District Court, 24 June 1983

Caged and hunted. Since 1986, these are the only forms of existence Brenden Abbott has known. Up until 1998, he had spent almost 2300 days on the run from police, in an investigation which began as a single file at the Perth Armed Robbery Squad office and grew to involve every operational police officer in Australia. Another five years were spent inside maximum security prisons, where escape was his single-minded pursuit.

More than anything, he hated being locked up. When free, Abbott traversed the nation with a regularity and breadth unheard of in the world of violent crime. And it was travel — as well as his much-vaunted intelligence and methodical nature — that was the key to his success as a fugitive. There were suburban apartments and houses, and an assortment of storage sheds and hideaways scattered across the country, but these served only as a base for operations — there was no fixed address.

As Abbott's horizons expanded, so did his audience. There were dozens of suspected armed robberies — few of them confirmed — in almost all the state capital cities from 1989 to 1998. He was a violent criminal on a truly national scale, which led to an unprecedented public profile.

The media, detecting a whiff of anti-hero from the start, followed his career with glee and coined a phrase for every occasion — the Drop-In Bandit, the Postcard Bandit, the Speedway Captain and, in the end, simply Australia's Most Wanted.

The title of latter day Ned Kelly was also applied, and in some ways, it was appropriate. In the 1870s, Kelly and his gang murdered three police officers in a shoot-out, and Kelly subsequently eluded the Victorian Police for 18 months. The newly developed media of the day turned him into a legend, in the same way that their modern counterparts have done to Abbott. A brilliant bushman and horse rider, the iron helmet, the famous last words ('Ah well, I suppose it has come to this. Such is life.'), his love of the bush — these elements made him the quintessential Australian outlaw.

But recently, some historians have cast doubt on Kelly's image. The *Oxford Companion to Australian History* describes Kelly as 'only a fair bushman and horseman' whose 'offences were few'. Others have disputed his reported last words, saying he was misquoted.

Abbott's image was also hard to quantify, and was muddled by myth and rumour. There was no doubting his success as a fugitive, but it was easy to make claims and allegations about a man who didn't want to be found.

Over the years, the tales became wilder and harder to believe. The Postcard Bandit — his most famous title and central to his image — was completely baseless. In 1990, police hunting Abbott seized holiday snaps from a getaway car and an accomplice's hideout. *The West Australian* published the pictures and reported the facts, but also remarked: 'Detectives believe some of the photos were to be sent to their associates as a cheeky reminder of how good life on the run could be.'

No one quite knows who first misinterpreted this statement — mistakenly or otherwise — but within a year, other media outlets were putting a different spin on the story. Now, he was the larrikin outlaw who robbed banks all over the country, taunting his pursuers. The Postcard Bandit was born.

Doubts would arise when a bemused Abbott tried to set the record straight after his recapture. But few took any notice. It spoiled the legend. And it was in the paper and on TV — it had to be true.

The postcards weren't the only tall tale. Abbott's infamy reached a point where he was an automatic suspect — at least for the media — in virtually every bank robbery in Australia. Even the cases in which he was considered a genuine suspect by police numbered more than 40, which, in one particular two-year period, meant he would have had to rob a bank every two months.

But myths and mistakes aside, the truth about Brenden Abbott would prove far more fascinating. On a cultural level he is stereotypically Australian, to the point of seeming like a product of central casting. His favourite pastimes as a fugitive are outback travel, watching the Australian cricket team in action and restoring old Holdens to their former glory. His favourite outfit is an Akubra hat, shorts and a T-shirt. Witty one-liners are delivered under dangerous circumstances in a friendly Aussie drawl littered with ockerisms. He also likes an occasional beer, grows his own marijuana and hates hard drugs.

But as a criminal, Abbott is anything but a stereotype, his casual demeanour and appearance masking intelligence and cunning. His status as a professional and successful bank robber alone was enough to set him apart from the average modern villain who has given crime a bad name. Corrupt businessmen and politicians, paedophiles and stalkers, mass killers and domestic murderers — front page crime in the nineties makes for unpleasant reading.

In comparison, Brenden Abbott appeared to be a lovable rogue, especially to a nation that loves a good villain. Anyone who robbed banks and stuck it up the coppers was all right by them. But who could they believe? Was Brenden Abbott a criminal mastermind and an Australian icon, or simply the product of media exaggeration and police paranoia? Only two groups of people — the police who hunted him and the family who raised him — know the answer.

Abbott was born in Footscray, in Melbourne, on 8 May 1962, the third of five children produced from the turbulent marriage of Brian and Thelma Abbott. His birth certificate bears the name 'Brenden James Abbott', but for most of his criminal career his Christian name was spelt 'Brendan' or 'Brendon' by the authorities and media. He never bothered to correct it — any name that caused confusion could only benefit a man who used dozens of aliases.

His immediate family — his parents and siblings Janet, David, Diane and Glenn — have rarely spoken at length with either the police or the media about Abbott's life of crime, and they refused all the author's requests for interviews. Bitter experience had taught some of them that talking could lead to disastrous consequences.

However, in April 1998 — while their brother was on the run yet again — his two sisters and older brother gave an intriguing insight into their family's early years in an interview with journalist Frank Robson, published in *Good Weekend*.

'You've got to understand the sort of family we come from,' Janet Kingdom, nee Abbott, told Robson. 'Whatever hardships they put on us, we've already suffered worse things as children. Our father was the cruellest, meanest man I've ever known. After he split, we kids basically raised ourselves, and Mum went further into her drinking and gambling.'

Their mother's habits conflicted with their father's attitude to alcohol and parental discipline. In 1971, three years after the youngest of the five, Glenn, was born, the Abbotts moved from Melbourne to Alice Springs and the family soon fell apart.

Brian Abbott returned to Melbourne and disappeared from their lives. Up until then, the family had been well cared for financially, but the sisters were never sure of what he did for a living. 'But we always had new cars and furniture, the best of everything,' Janet says.

They remembered him as being well-dressed and occasionally charming, and Brenden would later develop his own theories on what his father did for a living.

David remained in the Northern Territory, where he built his own life and family. Thelma and the other children moved on, eventually settling in Tom Price, in Western Australia's north-west. But without financial security and his father's controlling

Thelma moved the family to Perth to be closer to him, and the working-class inner eastern suburbs became their permanent home. Brenden and Glenn, who always followed his brother's lead, became adept young thieves in their early teens, and both were soon in trouble with the law. Brenden recorded his first convictions for breaking, entering and stealing at age 14; Glenn was just nine.

One of Abbott's teachers remembers him as an under-achiever who was only interested in school when it involved cricket. At other times, he had an uncanny knack of disappearing without trace. He had his fair share of teenage female admirers, and a girlfriend of one of his young partners in crime remembers one interlude clearly. She had always liked Brenden, and had threatened to sleep with him if her boyfriend didn't stop cheating on her. Finally, it became too much, and they did the deed in the lounge room of her parents' house. But they were interrupted by her angry mother, an imposing figure who was a prison officer.

'Brenden was mortified. I don't think he was ever as scared as he was at that moment. He grabbed his pants and bolted,' she remembers. The girl later broke off contact with the group, when Abbott began leading them into more serious crime.

In later years, there would be no shortage of women who were attracted to him, supporting the theory that dangerousness can be a powerful aphrodisiac. There were regulars who corresponded with him in jail, and a string of casual girlfriends while on the run.

Janet and Diane made a decision to escape their brother's growing influence, and in 1986 they moved to Cairns with their own young families. The eight members of the family were eventually cast to the four winds, spread across three states and a territory. But they remained loyal to Brenden, and most would come under close scrutiny from police as his criminal record grew.

'I wasn't a model citizen,' Janet says. 'The family mentality was "us against them", and anything we did was justified.'

Friends from his teenage years remember Abbott as an easy-going mate who enjoyed a good time. He loved fast cars from an early age and loved tinkering about under bonnets. And as his stealing habits grew, Abbott made himself popular by offloading goods in what became known as 'Brenden sales'. He would gather together an assortment of clothes and electrical goods and then sell them cheaply within his circle of friends. It was perhaps the closest he came to fulfilling yet another media tag — but 'mate's rates' on stolen goods hardly qualified him as Robin Hood.

By 1980, Abbott had compiled a respectable criminal record for an 18-year-old, ranging from stealing and breaking and entering to disorderly conduct, unlawful damage and using threatening language. There was even a $50 good behaviour date. He had dropped by a mate's place in north-east suburban Bassendean for a few drinks. They soon became bored and decided to head into the city looking for action. Abbott's Torana was almost out of petrol, so a resourceful mate, 17-year-old Ray Skehan, crept down the street and milked some fuel from a car parked in a nearby front yard. But he got greedy and was caught by the owner when he returned for more, resulting in a stealing charge and fine.

Abbott was livid when police decided to charge him with receiving, based on the fact that the stolen petrol was put into his car, and he contested the charge. In December 1980, shortly after Skehan received a summons to appear as a witness in the case, Abbott dropped by his Dianella home.

'Brenden Abbott came over to my house in Jarot Place and asked me what I was going to say in court,' Skehan later told another court. 'I told him I was going to say the petrol went into his car and he told me to say that I had spilt the petrol running back from the house down the road.'

Later, waiting outside the Beaufort Street court to give evidence, Abbott approached him again and repeated the demand. Skehan went inside and tried to back out of his previous statement. But the prosecuting sergeant and detective handling the case were having none of it, and he went back outside to break the news to Abbott.

'He shook. He just started getting angry, because I couldn't say what he wanted me to say,' Skehan later testified. 'He shook his fist and just tapped me on the arm with a finger and then he got called into court.'

Scared, Skehan told the court that Abbott had been unaware the petrol had been put in his car. This effectively destroyed the prosecution case and Abbott was found not guilty.

In subsequent months, Abbott actually began to steer his life away from crime, but the police weren't prepared to let the receiving charge rest. In April 1981, Warwick detective Brian Brennan arrested him at a construction site at Wagerup, south of Perth, and then interviewed him at the nearby Waroona police station. Ray Skehan and Craig Wilson, another man who had been at the Bassendean house that night, had both been charged with conspiring to pervert the course of justice. Brennan told Abbott he faced the same charge, and outlined the allegations. 'What have you got to say?'

'I'm not denying anything, but I'm not admitting anything either. I want to talk to my lawyer.'

Abbott was learning to play the game, but he was still worried. 'Do you think I'll go to jail?' he asked the detective.

'There's every possibility.'

'Well, I've got a good job. I'm doing well. I look like going on to the scrapers [on the construction site] in a couple of weeks and I want to show the magistrate that I want to settle down and work.'

But Abbott landed in jail before the case even reached court. In August 1981, he was sentenced to 18 months for stealing and stripping cars and breach of probation and, at the age of 19, was sent to Fremantle Prison.

For even the most hardened young criminal, life within the limestone walls was a shock. The prison was a throwback to the convict era in which it was built. In the 1860s, the inmates were hard and conditions harder. Little had changed.

Abbott was released in a few months, but he was a changed man. Up until that point, friends say, he wasn't much more than a wild teenager. Now he was moody and introspective, and crime soon became a full-time pursuit, with the tricks learned and contacts made in Fremantle Prison providing the perfect grounding.

In March 1982, he faced trial over the conspiracy charge, standing by the story that he didn't know the petrol had been put in his car. A nervous Ray Skehan took the stand and related the events of the night and Abbott's subsequent alleged threats. After he admitted his perjury, the prosecutor asked why he had lied. 'Because I was frightened. Frightened of Brenden going after me or beating me up.' His testimony was enough. Somehow, Abbott's desire for a city drive had led to the prospect of a lengthy jail term.

His lawyer, Brian Singleton, was also mystified, he told the jury. 'You have before you a young man who is charged with an offence which is not often brought before the courts. Certainly in 22 years it is the first one in which I have been involved.'

A few weeks later, Judge Ackland delivered sentence, noting

that the offence was one of 'considerable gravity'. But just as he had finished telling Abbott that he could see 'no alternative but to sentence you to a term of imprisonment', Abbott's lawyer, Ross Lonnie, finally arrived, breathless. He had managed to find something that the lawyers who later defended Abbott could only dream of — a character witness.

'Sir, I apologise to the court for being late. I have in the court Mr John MacKay, who was on the Parole Board, who knows Abbott, who is prepared to give evidence on his behalf and I wonder if you would . . .'

'Very well.'

'Mr MacKay, what is your present occupation?'

'I am the director of the Western Australia Wheat Council.'

'What was your position when you came to know Abbott?'

'I was the executive director of the YMCA in Perth.'

'How did you come to know Abbott?'

'It was through the Community Youth Support Scheme, of which I was the chairman . . . Brenden was under my care at that time and did a tremendous job in carrying out the community service order.'

'You actually supervised him?'

'That's right, yes.'

'How do you say he performed?'

'He performed very well. I think I was able to gain his confidence and to see that there was a potential for the young man. My purpose in being here today is to speak for him because I believe that, with support — which I am prepared to give at any time now and later when he is released — I can get him back into society. I am acting as a sort of friend and counsellor now and have visited him at Fremantle Prison.'

'Have you seen him since he has been in prison?'

'Yes.'

'What is the effect that prison has had on him?'

'I think it has had a very damaging effect on him from a developmental point of view. He is a realist and I am a realist in the sense that I know he is breaking the law but I believe the potential . . .'

'You think it has had a good effect on him in that he is aware of the repercussions if he breaks the law?'

'The salutary effect, yes, but in terms of any long-term time I think it would be bad for him as it is, I believe, for any young man his age. I believe that certainly he has gained from the loss of freedom but I think there is a time when you know that can go too far, particularly at his age now of about 19 years.'

'You have heard what His Honour said — that Abbott has a long record and the matter is a serious matter — yet with that you still say he would benefit by not going to prison further.'

'For any further time? I would be inclined to agree with that.

I believe that he needs friends and I believe he has the right attitude in the discussions I have had with him. I have even talked with the young lady whom he is hoping to marry. I believe her effect on him will be beneficial too in terms of his rehabilitation.'

Never before — and never again — would such a passionate advocate take the stand on Abbott's behalf. In hindsight, John MacKay's pleas and hopes seem almost naive. But he was one of the first to recognise Abbott's genuine intelligence and potential. He simply wanted to steer him in the right direction before it was too late.

'In spite of those favourable remarks, I can see no alternative but to sentence you to be imprisoned,' Judge Ackland told Abbott. 'I sentence you to be imprisoned for three years. Of that, you must serve 12 months before you become eligible for parole. There is no reason in law why that sentence should not have been added to the sentence which you are now serving but you are yet young and it appears to me that to add three years to the term of 18 months which you are now serving would be to impose too heavy a burden on you. I therefore direct that the sentence just imposed will be served concurrently with the sentences you are now serving.'

Effectively, he wouldn't serve any extra time in jail as a result of being found guilty. But the experience still left Abbott with a bitter taste in his mouth, and he appealed on principle.

In August 1982, he was vindicated by the Court of Criminal Appeal, who agreed that the trial judge had erred on a number of issues in his instructions to the jury. Yet, within two months of that decision, he was in trouble again, making his first foray into serious violent crime.

Abbott and three mates planned a bag snatch on employees of a Perth restaurant, Miss Maud's, just before they arrived at a bank to deposit the day's takings. The idea was workable, but the result was amateurish.

One pair successfully grabbed the takings — $12 775 in cash and cheques — and fled through the nearby Supreme Court Gardens, where the others were waiting to make a quick getaway. But they were caught, cold, when they were spotted and reported to police soon after by a witness to the crime.

Abbott was released on bail, knowing that a jail term was inevitable. He would submit a rare plea of guilty, choosing to stay and face the music — his days as a fugitive still several years off. Later, he resolved to never again accept a legal defeat without a fight.

The decision to plead guilty hadn't been easy, as his lawyer, Ross Lonnie, explained to the Perth District Court in May 1983 after requesting a pre-sentence report.

'Yes, thank you, Mr Lonnie. The prisoner is just 20,' Judge Hammond commented.

'Yes, sir.'

'I think, sadly, 21 the day after tomorrow?'

'Yes, I am afraid so, sir. He has of course been out on bail and I think it speaks well of him that he is here today. I have explained to him that you probably would not continue that . . . I think he would be breached in any event with the entering of the plea. He is on parole at the moment, you see.'

Seven weeks after Abbott volunteered to spend his 21st birthday in Fremantle Prison, an apologetic Lonnie delivered sentencing submissions to the court on his behalf.

'I have had the distinction of acting for Brenden over the last three or four years and have represented him in most of these matters which have been before the court. We are very sorry that we are here before the court and that he has reoffended whilst on parole.'

He went on to repeat the effusive praise of John MacKay, pointing out that Abbott had responded well under the right supervision while on parole.

'Yes, but really it is not a question of probation being imposed. It is a minimum term,' Judge Hammond told him.

'That is why I am making those submissions. I do not for one minute think that you are going to be granting probation. What I am saying is that he obviously has a bad record, he has done something when he was on parole. But I am asking you to consider a minimum term which is not going to leave him in there too long, but gives him a reward, gives him an opportunity to have something to look forward to. There is good in Abbott and I would like him to have the opportunity of coming out as soon as possible.'

Judge Hammond was unimpressed. 'When one looks at your antecedents and your criminal history, there is very little encouragement to be gained, notwithstanding all that has been said on your behalf.' He sentenced him to four years, with a 22-month minimum.

Abbott returned to Fremantle Prison and the die was cast. Soon, police would receive a proper introduction to his emerging criminal skills.

After his release on parole in 1985, Abbott didn't return immediately to crime; instead, he travelled to the north of the state and worked as a casual labourer. But when he returned to Perth, breaking and entering soon became his full-time occupation.

Sergeant Jeff Beaman, a Western Australian detective who would follow Abbott's criminal career closely, remembers a young thief who had decided the only way to fight the system was to beat it. 'His MO [*modus operandi*] developed to the point where he was knocking holes in walls with sledgehammers after casing the place and checking for areas not covered by alarms,' Beaman said. His speciality was electrical stores, and jobs would be tailored to suit the specific needs of his 'customers'.

Abbott and Beaman first crossed paths late in 1986, while the detective was at the north suburban Nollamara CIB. They had received a tip-off that a young criminal, David Stabback, was in possession of stolen goods. When they executed a search warrant on his home early one morning, an Aladdin's cave of stolen goods was found, including scuba diving equipment, chainsaws, sheepskin covers, car stereos, a television, microwave, coffee table and washing machine. Stabback said he had received most of it from two brothers whom he feared — Brenden and Glenn Abbott.

Some of the stolen goods were from major break and enters, and Beaman and another detective, Sergeant Michael Bourke, began liaising with the Break Squad. One break-in had only just taken place, at a Homecraft store in the northern coastal suburb of Whitfords, on December 16. The thieves had made their initial entry through the roof, and then backed a stolen truck up to the rear roller door, loading it with electrical goods valued at $20 000.

After the raid on Stabback's home, another of his associates, David Knapp, came under scrutiny from the detectives. A Torana towing a trailer was seen leaving his home and delivering whitegoods and electrical items around the metropolitan area, including to one address already well known to police — 141 Surrey Road, Rivervale. It was home to Thelma Abbott, now Thelma Salmon after remarrying carpenter John Salmon in 1978. But things didn't work out and the marriage was eventually dissolved in 1987.

Brenden, who was driving the Torana, was watched as he unloaded a new Hoover washing machine and wheeled it into his mother's laundry. He was then followed to a unit in Ozone Parade, Scarborough, and at 6 am the next day, Beaman and Bourke were banging on the door, armed with a search warrant.

In a simultaneous raid by the Break Squad on the Rivervale address, a surprised Thelma Salmon had her new washing machine seized just as she was about to put in the first load.

At the Scarborough address the detectives found Abbott, his girlfriend Jacki Lord — also known as Rhonda Green — and another man not connected to the investigation. A search uncovered a freezer, hairdryer, food mixer, frying pan and iron, all brand-new.

'Where's this property come from, Brenden?' Bourke asked.

'Can't a man buy his girlfriend a Christmas present?'

'That's not what I asked. Where's it come from?'

'Why ask me? It's not my flat. I only came here last night.'

'Brenden, Rhonda and David have said I should ask you all about it.'

'I want to ring my lawyer.' Abbott grabbed a phone book and began dialling a number.

'Your lawyer is hardly likely to be in his office. It's 6.45,' Beaman pointed out helpfully.

Abbott became annoyed. 'Jacki, put on a tape. I want to record all this.' But they couldn't find a tape, and the detectives were happy to oblige.

'You can all go to the station and sort out who the property belongs to,' Bourke told them.

They returned to the old house which served as Nollamara CIB's base and Abbott was placed in an interview room. 'Brenden, all your clothes and papers are in the flat so it's obvious that you live there,' Bourke said.

'So? I live there now and again.'

'Before we speak to Rhonda or David, do you want to help us? All the gear that we have at your flat appears to have come from a break and enter at Homecraft at Whitfords two nights ago.'

'Rhonda and David are big enough to look after themselves. I'm not saying anything until my lawyer's here.'

'That will be arranged.'

Bourke left the room to speak to Rhonda, and a junior detective was given the task of watching Abbott.

'He was like a cat on a hot tin roof. He was looking around everywhere, and we were all worried he was going to try to bolt,' Beaman recalls.

Later, the young detective walked up to Beaman. 'How's it going?'

Not well, given that a toey prisoner now seemed to be unsupervised. 'Where's Abbott?' Beaman asked, knowing the answer seconds later when he heard the back door slam. Abbott, fit, was several backyards away in a matter of seconds. A search was mounted, but he was gone.

Abbott wisely avoided Perth as much as possible over the next few months, testing out his skills as a fugitive. He was still on parole, but for obvious reasons stayed out of contact with his parole officer, leading to suspension of his parole in January 1987 and its cancellation the following May. Jeff Beaman, meanwhile, joined the Break Squad where he continued to search for Abbott, whose name was still cropping up in investigations. Abbott would later say that his income from this period was derived from 'illegal matters', mostly involving the sale of cannabis.

He remained elusive until his dramatic arrest at Perth Airport on 4 June 1987. Later that day, Beaman finally got the opportunity to continue the interview that had been cut short

to you about the break at Homecraft at Whitfords last December.'

'There's not much I can say about that. You found some of the gear in my flat.'

'We searched your flat and several other places on December 16 and recovered about $3000 worth of property.'

'All the rest is gone now.'

'Where's it gone?'

'I never dropped anyone's name in. It's six months ago now. The property is gone. You'll never get it back.'

Beaman pressed on. 'As you know, Mark Reynolds [another mate Abbott had met while learning martial arts] and David Knapp have been charged with the offence. Your girlfriend Rhonda Green — or Jacki Lord as you know her — has been charged with receiving property that was in the flat. What do you want to say about that matter?'

'You tell me what they have said.'

Beaman began reading out their statements and Abbott listened, shaking his head. 'I've heard enough.'

'Is that the truth, what they have said?'

'Yeah, I'll have to cop that break. That's why I ran off that day. I knew you had me cold.'

'Do you wish to make a statement in relation to this matter?'

'No, I'll never go to paper. Can the charges against Jacki be dropped? She's not a crim. I'm the one who did the break. You've got me. You only charged her because I ran off.'

'She was charged because she admitted committing the offence.'

'Can you do anything about it?'

'No.'

'What about the washing machine I gave my mother? What will happen to her?'

'Did she know where it came from?'

'No, all I said to her was "Merry Christmas". She's innocent. You've got Knappy, Reynolds and me for the break. That's enough. If I hadn't kept any of the gear I would have been all right. Besides, this break doesn't worry me at all.'

No wonder — there was still the small matter of the Belmont robbery to be dealt with, and he was in a belligerent mood by the time Detective Sergeant Ian Brandis began the second interview that day.

'As you are no doubt aware, we are making inquiries regarding the Commonwealth Bank in Belmont,' he told Abbott.

'Good, but I can't help you.'

'We've received information that you were one of the persons involved.'

'Well, your information's not too good.'

'I've just been told that you had two bags at the airport which contained a large sum of money and a gun.'

'They're not my bags. I've never seen them before.'

'Where's your luggage, then?'

'I didn't have any.'

'Inquiries have been conducted at the Port Hedland Airport. A female staff member there stated that a man fitting your description purchased a ticket in the name of Applegate and weighed those two bags in to be checked.'

'She might be wrong. Everyone makes mistakes.'

But there was no mistaking the evidence found inside the bag, including personal papers and identification for Mark Anthony Mannion, an Abbott associate from Fremantle Prison. Abbott had used Mannion's birth certificate, driver's licence, TAFE card and tax return to hide his identity while on the run. There was also a birthday card inscribed, 'To Brenden, wishing you all the best and future happiness always. Love Always, Jacki. Happy Birthday 25.' Brandis held it up accusingly.

'So? There's more than one Brenden in the world,' Abbott responded.

'How many 25-year-old Brenden's with a girlfriend named Jacki?'

'There's a point,' he admitted.

'Is that money in the bag from the Commonwealth Bank?'

'I'm not sure.'

'What do you mean?'

'Just what I said.'

'The gun found in your luggage is one of many that was stolen from a Maddington gun shop and is the same calibre as the one fired during the bank robbery.'

'That may be so, but I'm not going to make your job easy for you.'

'Are you aware that we have arrested Peter Lievense?'

'What did he say to you?'

'He's told us that you went to his place the day before the robbery and borrowed a bag from him and when you took it back to him it had bundles of money in it.'

'I don't know what you expect me to say. I don't lag on anyone.'

'As I said before, the pistol found in your luggage was reported stolen from the Maddington gun shop. Can you explain how that came to be in your possession?'

'I didn't do the break on the gun shop.'

'Well how did the pistol get in your possession?'

Abbott summoned the correct legal terminology. 'I received it.'

'Who from?'

'You don't expect me to answer that, do you?'

'At the time of receiving it, did you know it was stolen?'

'Yes, but as I said before, I didn't take it.'

'Like I said before, the gun is the same calibre as the one fired during the robbery.'

'Well, it wasn't that one, and it was an accident anyway.'

'How do you know that, Brenden? Are you saying that you're involved in the robbery?'

'It certainly looks that way. You've got the gun and the money and a card in the bag.'

'Was the other person David Stabback?'

'Let's just talk about what I've done.'

'Brenden, I've told you before that I've received information that you and David Stabback did the robbery.'

Abbott had just about had enough. 'Look, you've got me for it. I'll cop my part, but I'm not saying anything about anyone else.

And I won't be signing anything. Let's get that straight right here and now.'

'There are still some things I want to ask you. For instance, the vehicle used in the robbery. Who took that from the yard?'

'You can charge me for that as well. I'll cop that too, but I'm not saying anything about anyone else.'

'In answer to my question, did you drive the car away from Skipper Mitsubishi?'

'Let's just say I was there and I was in it.'

'How much money is in the bag?'

'I don't know.'

'There was over $100 000 in the bag. What happened to the rest of it?'

'Whatever's there is all that I've got left.'

'What happened to the rest of it?'

'Whatever's in the bag is all that's left of my share.'

'How much is there?'

'I don't know.'

'Are you prepared to give me a statement about the receiving of the gun, the robbery of the bank and the taking of the Mitsubishi car?'

'No way. I've said enough. You've got enough to hang me anyway.'

'You'll be charged with the receiving of the gun, the unauthorised use of the car and the robbery on the bank. Do you understand that?'

'Yes.'

'Is there anything else you want to ask me?'

'Who dobbed me in?'

'You know I can't tell you that. Regarding the gun, the

Break Squad want to talk to you about that. They're handling that inquiry.'

'OK, but I only received it. I didn't do the break,' he stressed.

Beaman re-entered, and Abbott told him there were three .45s, two .357 Magnums, a .32 special, a .38 Smith and Wesson, an air pistol and a handful of target pistols taken in the gun shop break.

'How do you know all that if you didn't do the break?' Beaman asked.

'I saw all the guns laid out on the table.'

'Where have the rest of the guns gone?'

'There are about ten in the river. Four you will never get back. The .357 I might be able to get back but some money will have to change hands.'

'Where are the guns in the river?'

'I'll have to speak to someone first.'

'Why can't we get four back?'

'They were sold to people I don't know.'

'What about the .357?'

'I'll have to make a couple of phone calls to arrange money to change hands.'

'You said you received a gun?'

'Yeah, they're worth $1200 on the street.'

'Brenden, these guns in the river, are we going to be able to recover them?'

'I know you blokes have got a job to do, but I've got to look after my own interests.'

He was allowed to speak briefly with Stabback, and then took Beaman to the Garratt Road Bridge and pointed to where the weapons had been dumped. Beaman knew he would get

'I wish I'd never met you,' Abbott hissed as he was placed in handcuffs and removed from the court. 'Likewise,' Lievense thought. He later received a heavy-handed six-year jail term, reduced on appeal to two years with a nine-month minimum.

The day of the court appearance, Lievense was released on bail, bruised and regretful, his 15-year friendship with Abbott well and truly over. Abbott left the court building in a prison security van, with his hands cuffed, feet chained and his temper boiling. It was December 1, the first day of summer. Down at Fremantle Prison, the mercury and tension were also beginning to rise.

Chapter 4

Fremantle burns

'When the laggings are over,
And we've all done our time,
We'll be brothers together,
As brothers in crime.'

— Fremantle Prison graffiti

In Fremantle Prison, time stood still. Outside, the port had developed into a cosmopolitan city; but within the prison's limestone walls, little had changed since the 1850s. The cells were marginally better and the gallows no longer in use, but otherwise the conditions were the same as the architecture — early Victorian.

The prisoners spent 14 hours a day in their cells, with buckets for toilets and another inmate for company. In winter they shivered, in summer they sweltered, and cockroaches and mice abounded. High tension was the norm, and casual violence was common in the hopelessly overcrowded prison. Brenden and Glenn Abbott shared the hardships together, both spending a large portion of the 1980s in the prison. Glenn, now 19, had followed in his brother's footsteps, developing into a violent young career criminal.

The Western Australian government had been talking about building a new prison since 1971 — even now, plans were in place — but nothing ever quite seemed to get off the ground.

The prisoners had had enough and on January 4, a combination of circumstances and heat finally pushed them over the edge. The day began badly. After the 7 am unlock, a prisoner in Main Division became abusive when a guard told him to hurry up. A scuffle followed and the prisoner was moved to an observation cell in another division. Later in the day, prison authorities made a fateful decision to return him to the Main Division yard, and unwittingly lit an already short fuse. The prisoner, angry and upset, claimed to have been bashed by the guard and emotions were soon running high.

A series of meetings were held in Main Division and Two Division, and prisoners conferred via a tennis ball with a piece of paper stuffed in a slit. 'We want to know what's going on. We're out at the moment. Don't leave us posted. Reply straight away,' one note read.

'Two Division — hang on. Stay cool. We are in the process of deciding. Give us [until] 3.30 pm. We won't weaken. Just give us time.'

Prison officers became nervous. The temperature outside was around 40°C. Inside the prison, it was at least 10°C higher. The situation was going downhill fast, but a request for the feared Metropolitan Security Unit (MSU) to be mobilised was refused. Instead, the prisoners were to be fed and returned to their cells in an effort to calm the situation.

By mid-afternoon, an unusual silence had settled over the prison. At 4.15 pm, just as the meals were about to be served, prisoners began pouring in from the Three Division yard with shouts of 'Let's take 'em' and 'Go, go, go'. They overwhelmed the officers who had been about to serve the food, hurling metal plates and buckets of hot water, and attacking them first with fists, then with lumps of wood. Within five minutes, smoke was billowing from the roof of Three Division, as prisoners moved from cell to cell lighting fires. It was clear that they had no intention of returning to their current living conditions.

In the initial bloody confrontation, 15 prison officers were injured, including one who had been in the job just a few weeks. He was dragged, semi-conscious, into a cell and released for medical treatment within half an hour of the initial rush. Five other guards were surrounded by prisoners armed with timber and cornered in the yard. They were an insurance policy against the MSU and a bargaining chip in negotiations.

With about 130 prisoners now controlling a large section of the prison, Superintendent Ivor Knight made the response clear — any prisoner seen to assault a guard was to be shot. In a legendary display of no-nonsense courage at the height of the

advanced on a group of about 40 prisoners who were out of control. After telling them to get back in their cells and 'behave', he was set upon. He fought back, but was overcome and placed in a cell.

In between dodging rocks and other missiles, firefighters managed to save three-quarters of the prison's main building, but the damage bill was still put at well over $1 million.

Prisoners were posted on roofs as lookouts, passing intelligence on outside activities down to the ringleaders. Amid fears of a mass breakout, a huge police contingent surrounded the prison. As negotiation attempts — and threats of tear gas — continued, hundreds of pizzas were ordered in and the opposing sides settled in for an uneasy night.

Glenn Abbott played a key role in the 19-hour stand-off. He was later charged with six counts of deprivation of liberty over the taking of the hostages and one count of assault. Judge Heenan later found that he was 'one of the prisoners who entered the building at or shortly after the storming of the gate. It was a particularly bad type of assault. While armed with a piece of timber, he struck a prison officer twice across his back, shoulders and head while he was trying to escape after being set upon by several other prisoners. He desisted only when a more responsible person told him to do so. After the prisoners had gone into the exercise yard taking five of the hostages with them, his involvement continued. Still armed with a piece of wood, he spent a good deal of time with and around the officers and did his share of look-out duty from the roof of the shed.'

But his older brother's role in the proceedings is less clear.

Brenden Abbott has always maintained there was a case of mistaken identity over the assaults he was charged with — and it was true that at times there was a remarkable likeness between him and his younger brother. But in court, prosecutor Ron Davies would describe Brenden as 'one of the stormtroopers' who was, 'in every sense, in the forefront of the most violent activities that occurred upon the initial rush'.

'The assaults were bad. The first involved him pushing a grille gate against the prison officer who was stationed behind it, and holding him there while he was punched repeatedly by another prisoner. The second assault occurred shortly afterwards on an upper level of the building. After Abbott and another prisoner confronted an officer, Abbott hit him twice with a piece of wood. The blows were aimed at the officer's head or face, but he took them mainly on one of his hands.

'In the exercise yard, he was one of those near the prison officers at an early stage, forming a barrier between them and the main bulk of the prisoners. He was still armed with a lump of wood. When police officers arrived on the bank overlooking the yard, he joined other prisoners in yelling abuse at them. Later, he took his turn as a look-out on the roof of the shed in the yard and at other times, helped the prisoners to get up onto the roof.'

There was no doubting Abbott's involvement at many points, but the events were chaotic and violent, and few have ever agreed on exactly what happened that afternoon. Either way, Abbott still included it on the list of grudges and complaints that would encourage him to pursue freedom.

In the wake of the riot, the prisoners made three demands — access to the media to air their complaints, personal interviews with senior prison department executives, and a guarantee of no physical repercussions for the prisoners involved. But the authorities would only agree to the last, and by the next morning the prisoners had other, more pressing, concerns. One prison officer was exchanged for plastic rubbish bins filled with baked beans and toast, and a second was handed over for two cartons of cigarettes. Late in the morning, the remaining three were released after the Police Minister, Gordon Hill, issued a message via a radio broadcast.

The prisoners surrendered, but they eventually got what they wanted. A report into the riot found that the conditions in the prison had made an uprising virtually inevitable and recommended that the facility be immediately upgraded. In 1991, Fremantle Prison was decommissioned after the opening of the new maximum security facility, Casuarina. But the careful restoration of the damaged section and the prison's historical value meant it was never destined for the bulldozers. Now, thousands of tourists pass through its gates on daily tours — its combination of beauty and horror-filled history an endless source of fascination.

In the prison's history, only one escapee is believed to have never been returned to its custody — Brenden Abbott. Or did he return? On 22 November 1992, while Abbott was on the run, a signature was left in a visitors' book which differed from the usual tourist remarks: '*Name*: B. Abbett. *Address*: Nowhere you'd find! *Remarks*: Great to come back and not have to escape.' Handwriting tests were conducted, but nothing was conclusive. And with former prison guards running tours, it seemed unlikely he would have taken the risk. But no one was ever quite sure.

Over the next two years, Brenden Abbott spent more time in courtrooms than do most lawyers. In addition to the mind-numbing four-month riot case, which became known simply as 'The Circus', Abbott also sat through three trials and an appeal.

The court appearances began six days after the riot ended, when high-profile Western Australian lawyer Richard Utting complained of difficulties in preparing Abbott's defence over the Whitfords break and enter. His cell had been burnt out in the fire, and notes that the budding jailhouse lawyer had compiled on the case had been destroyed. The case was adjourned, and it would be over a year before it finally reached trial.

In March 1988, a jury was disbelieving of Abbott's version of the Belmont robbery. He claimed that some of the cash found in his bag had been given to him by David Stabback to settle a drug debt. And it was a mysterious Maori man called Kiwi who had robbed the bank — not Abbott. He was sentenced to ten years, added to the two years he still owed the parole board. No minimum term was set, and Judge Smith told Abbott that until he grew up, there was little hope of parole being considered. 'Thank you. You are a real gentleman,' Abbott replied.

Later in the year, 'The Circus' commenced. With a cast of 19 lawyers, 20 accused men, a 6500-page report and a budget of $3 million, it was the state's biggest, longest and most expensive criminal trial.

Each day, a convoy of police and security vehicles would travel the Fremantle–Perth route to the court, where the prisoners were placed in a specially built glass dock. As the lawyers waded through the mountain of evidence, the inmates played cards, drew pictures, rattled their chains and, at times, laughed and joked.

The lighter moments were rare, but memorable. After newspapers reported Judge Heenan's singing talents, the defendants waltzed into the dock singing 'Danny Boy'. And when one prisoner wanted to complain about an alleged assault by a guard, he walked into the courtroom naked and took his seat. He then left quickly, having made his point, before the judge could order him from the court.

The monotony of the trial and the intense security measures often led to tension. Each day began with the prisoners being woken at 5.30 am and undergoing several strip searches during their journey to and from the court.

Finally, in December, an emotional jury returned verdicts on a total of 143 charges after deliberating for eight days. Two prisoners were found not guilty of all charges, and only three were convicted on all the charges they faced. Glenn Abbott received a total of four years, while Brenden received six years. This was later reduced to four years by the Court of Criminal Appeal, who ruled that it was 'too much' for a man of his age.

In March the following year, Abbott finally went on trial over the Whitfords break and enter. He took the stand and explained that there had been a terrible misunderstanding. He claimed to have had nothing to do with the raid on the electrical store, and had just been doing a favour for some mates. He had dropped by David Knapp's home in Sorrento one morning to pick up a washing machine he had bought for his mother. They needed some other items delivered and he had agreed to help out. He was being similarly selfless, he said, when he fled the police station.

'On the way to the police station from the flat, Detective Bourke said to me . . . because I was quite surprised as to how they knew about me having those appliances at my home . . .

I asked him about it and they said they had my mum's place under surveillance and they watched me pull in there the day before with the washing machine and followed me to the flat. So when I got to Nollamara police station they left me in a room. I left to ring up my mother and hopefully to get my brother to get rid of the washing machine. I didn't want my mother getting in trouble with police.'

'Why didn't you return to the police station?' he was asked.

'I didn't want to face the drama.'

He made an impression on the jury, who remained deadlocked after six hours and were discharged without reaching a verdict.

But the DPP wasn't prepared to give up. It was an open and shut case — he'd admitted his guilt to two detectives, part of the haul of goods was found at his house, and two other men had already been convicted. They'd get him next time.

In March 1989, Abbott faced trial again and stuck with the same story. Again, he explained his decision to escape, adding that he thought his brother had been involved with David Knapp and Mark Reynolds. 'It's quite obvious that my brother was up to no good with these two chaps and I think it was just the right thing to do . . . to warn him what's been happening.'

'So that's why you left?'

'As I say, it's not the main reason. I was really worried about my mother, and also Glenn's interests.'

Judge Williams spelt out the case to the jury, adding that it came down to a matter of which witnesses they believed — prosecution or defence. Again, they couldn't decide.

On May 5, the DPP threw in the towel and withdrew the charge of breaking and entering. It was an impressive legal

wanted to escape, it would have to be before then. Fremantle was secure, but it was old and still less than state-of-the-art despite the repairs. There were weaknesses which could be exploited. And still fresh in Abbott's memory, before the harsh reality of prison, was the 'good life' he had briefly tasted. Now he wanted more.

Chapter 5

Summer holiday

'Two fellas in the car. One is bald, about 35 . . . They've got a firearm. They've fired about three shots at us.'
— Police radio transmission, Perth, 19 December 1989

The cell search earlier in the week had been a close call. The guards found plenty, and it stuffed up some serious escape plans.

But not Brenden Abbott's. He still had his overalls and prison guard's cap, specially made in the tailor workshop of Fremantle Prison. And no one had noticed that one of the window bars — high up on one of the workshop's walls and obscured from the guard's office — had been cut through.

The guard glanced at his watch. It was around 3 o'clock on a sleepy Friday afternoon — 24 November 1989. His seven charges were working quietly away. Now that the problems earlier in the week were out of the way, it was a good time to catch up on some paperwork. He slipped into the office and sat down.

Immediately, the workshop burst into life. Several inmates pushed a fridge under the window, while three others pulled on overalls and caps. The first was William Monaghan, a member of the right-wing Australian Nationalist Movement, who was on remand over the murder of a fellow member. The second was Aaron Reynolds (no relation to Mark Reynolds), a tattoo-covered young career criminal who had bashed a supermarket employee with an iron bar during a robbery. The third was Abbott.

Prison guard disguises in place, they clambered onto the fridge. The adrenalin was pumping now and seemed to make it easier to pull back the stubborn iron bar. It wasn't a wide gap, and squeezing through seemed to take an eternity. The steepled roofs of the prison buildings provided good cover, and they moved quickly to an adjacent office roof.

The overalls and caps were a necessary precaution. The riot had hit the guards hard, and an escape attempt wouldn't be met with good humour. Planting a seed of doubt in their minds could mean the difference between freedom and the mortuary.

The trio bounded from roof to roof, and were finally spotted from the prosecutor's office window as they leapt between buildings. Abbott and Reynolds were fit men. Monaghan, apparently, was not. He failed to make a three-metre leap to a building near the prison's western outer wall and fell five metres. Prison officers found him, looking sheepish, in the small alley soon after.

But his cohorts fared better, reaching the outer wall and dropping to freedom. With a jarring thud, they hit the ground and sprinted to a waiting car. An intensive search was mounted, but there was nothing.

Abbott was gone. And he had no intention of coming back.

Chasing men you've already locked up isn't a favoured task of the average detective. And the expletives would have rolled thick and fast over at the Armed Robbery Squad office that day. It didn't take a genius to work out what came next: stick-ups, and lots of them. But mixed with the anger was also some grudging respect. In naming the subsequent operation, they deployed the full weight of their constabulary wit. Elmer Fudd, they called it. The hunt for Wabbit.

Indeed, Abbott and Reynolds were holed up — in a hotel, taking in views of Perth's Scarborough Beach for a few days. But they couldn't stay. They were all over the papers and TV. Armed and dangerous, the cops were saying. But we'll catch them.

For five days, they laid low. Then, on November 29, a simple but effective three-part operation was executed. It opened at the Max Williams gun shop in Subiaco early in the morning. A piece of the tin roof was folded back and two shotguns, a Mossberg and a Winchester, were stolen. A brief stop at the Morley Shopping Centre car park: Holden Commodore stolen. The clincher: ANZ Bank, Innaloo Shopping Centre, mid-afternoon. Second car left nearby. Commodore parks near front entrance. Two men enter — overalls, balaclavas, shotguns. The larger man takes centre stage, ordering the staff and customers to the floor. An employee reaches for an alarm button. He threatens to shoot her. Reynolds is nervous, unsure of his role. A teller overhears him whisper to an elderly customer: 'Don't worry, I won't hurt you or any of the kids.' They grab $6500. Exit bank, dump Commodore. Operation complete.

The pressure was on now and Abbott knew it.

'More hold-ups feared with escapees at large', *The West Australian* warned on December 1. 'Police fear that two prison

will commit further hold-ups,' the paper reported.

'Detectives said yesterday that the convicted armed robbers who escaped from Fremantle Prison last week could use stolen firearms in a series of desperate robberies.

'Detective Sergeant Garry Annetts said, "These men are desperate and dangerous and should not be approached in any circumstances".'

It was definitely time to make a move. But Abbott's options were limited by a cash shortage and the lack of an established support network. Staying on the run only became easier for him with time and planning. A few days in the bush would give him time to think.

On December 7, while the staff were distracted, Reynolds jumped into an F100 utility, its keys left in the ignition, at a Victoria Park car yard. It was a big vehicle and they filled it well: two bikes, camping and fishing gear, beer, food. Shorts and T-shirts, sunglasses and caps. A camera for those special moments. Just two blokes on a summer fishing trip — apart from the guns, ammunition, scanners, balaclavas, and lock picking equipment, which they tested on the F100.

Heading south, they passed through the small town of Dwellingup, about 110 kilometres from Perth. The pair drove slowly past the police station. Abbott couldn't resist. He pulled to a stop. Reynolds strolled over and leaned casually against the fence. With the police station sign in the background, Abbott captured the moment: Reynolds, with cheesy grin. Coppers, with no idea.

And it wasn't the only picture. Over the next few days, at a bush campsite, they honed their photography skills: Reynolds, cheesy grin again, with bulging wallet; Abbott enjoying an Emu Export; Reynolds playing with shotgun shells; Abbott waving scanners around. Boys' Own stuff. And compared with Fremantle Prison, it was a life of leisure.

Their only moment of danger came when they tried to catch some marron — the local freshwater crayfish — in the Blackwood River. It wasn't marron season and a fisheries inspector demanded to see their ID. Abbott was cool, playing the embarrassed citizen instead of the desperate escapee. He handed over a false driver's licence, took the infringement with good grace, and the danger passed as quickly as it had arisen.

But they couldn't stay in the sticks forever. The money was going to run out. The pair returned to Perth, and on December 12, Reynolds stole a Mitsubishi Cordia turbo in Scarborough, then a Toyota LandCruiser in Victoria Park the next day. On December 14, they decided it was time to cash up.

As they discussed their plan — this time it would be a TAB, a softer target — Reynolds took the plunge. He wanted to impress his older accomplice. 'I can handle it this time, BJ. You wait in the car.' Abbott didn't mind. He always encouraged young talent.

They started by swiping a Commodore from the Karrinyup Shopping Centre, a ten-minute drive north of the city, then drove to the Whitfords TAB, a few kilometres further north. Reynolds charged in, balaclava in place, waving a shotgun wildly. He looked fearsome, but didn't feel it. The terrified staff later commented on his nervousness. They handed over $4000 and it took some time to convince him there was no more.

Again, the pair escaped without a hitch. But how long could it last?

'What was the rego?'

'6IZ. He's heading south on the freeway. We're just approaching Warwick Road turn-off.'

Abbott headed straight for the nearest exit. Suburban streets were an easier place to shake off pursuit.

'Sierra 530, he's just gone on the off-ramp.'

'Which off-ramp? Warwick Road?'

'Roger, D. Warwick Road off-ramp.'

'Roger. You still in pursuit?'

'Roger.'

'Speed?'

'140.'

But the van was no match for the turbo.

'You still got him in sight, Sierra 530?'

'Negative mate. We've lost him. We're heading east on Warwick Road. He's nowhere in sight.'

Probationary Constable Phil Milne and Senior Constable Dave Briggs had been listening in on the chase, but they had other things on their minds. They had just left Warwick police station on a sombre journey. An off-duty police officer had died in an accident that night. They were supposed to be picking up relatives to identify the body.

But Abbott's choice of route ended that. Suddenly, the chase was on top of them. Milne, the driver, threw his Coke out the window and turned off Warwick Road. 'Sierra 538, we've got him in Dorchester . . . doing about 130.'

Abbott swung a hard right and tore down Springvale Drive, throwing it around the corner in an attempt to reverse direction. At the next corner, he tried again, turning right into Raasay Place a few hundred metres on. This time, he lost control and the Cordia screeched to a halt, stalling.

'What's the traffic conditions and speed?'

'About 120 . . . '

Briggs' voice lifted an octave: 'He's lost it!'

The patrol car rounded the corner and the two cars brushed, coming to rest side by side. Briggs, in the passenger seat of the patrol car, peered at the shaven-headed figure a few feet away. '. . . TA [traffic accident] with us . . . '

'Sierra 538, where did he lose the vehicle?'

Abbott tried desperately to restart the Cordia. Reynolds jumped from the passenger side, leaned over the roof, levelled a shotgun at the patrol car and pulled the trigger. It missed. 'Could've hit them if I wanted,' he later pouted.

It bought some time. Abbott got the motor started, threw the Cordia into reverse and headed back up the hill. Milne did the same and turned to look through the rear window. He saw a

Forensics would later recover light birdshot from the rear window. A heavier gauge . . . well, that would have been a different story. Without the impact of the shot, it didn't seem real.

Right now, anger at being used for target practice blocked out all other thoughts. Milne barely paused as they reversed and continued the chase. Briggs grabbed the radio and managed to get in a few words over the anxious VKI operator. '. . . shooting at us . . .'

'VKI: Repeat?'

Reynolds let another one go as the Cordia rounded the corner into Dorchester. Briggs reached for the revolver on his right hip. But he wasn't used to simultaneous gun battles and high-speed chases. The seatbelt buckle, high speed and wrenching corners conspired against him.

'In Springvale heading back up towards Dorchester. Two fellas in the car. One is bald, about 35 years of age. They've got a firearm. They've fired about three shots at us.'

The Division 79 crews almost spilled their coffee in the rush. They knew who that sounded like.

'VKI: Any Delta vehicles to attend?'

'Delta 4 on the way.'

'Delta 8 as well.'

'Sierra 538: Turned right into Dorchester heading back towards Beach Road.'

'VKI: Roger. Sit right back, sit right back. Keep the vehicle in sight but sit back. Take all care, Sierra 538. Direction?'

'Dorchester, still heading towards Beach Road. Appeared to be either a shotgun or something big. He's turned left. Just fired another shot at us.'

'VKI: Yeah, which way's he gone? Left on what road?'

'Dugdale Street. We're turning left into another street. Hang on a sec.'

The patrol car swung into Glenmere Road and followed it around. But Abbott hadn't. He chose the first left, Addison Way, and then ducked into a small cul de sac, Adela Place.

By now, the area was swarming with patrol cars and divisional vans. A perimeter was thrown up. The Warwick police complex was only a few hundred metres away, and foot patrols were quickly dispatched.

'VKI: Sierra 538, did you pick up the numerals on that vehicle?'

'Negative. We were too busy ducking.'

But they kept looking. It wasn't long before the patrol car swung into Addison Way and paused at the entrance to Adela Place. The Cordia was at the end, passenger door ajar, lights off. The street lights were off too, the window tinting was dark and the Cordia had rear louvres. Ominously, the houses in a semi-circle around it had large brick fences.

'Sierra 538, we've got the vehicle. 7IZ 171. We're in Adela Place. It appears as though they have abandoned the vehicle. We're just going to sit here at the moment until we get some help.'

'Delta 4: Get someone to check the vehicle. Make sure if the firearm's still there. If not . . . all care to be taken, mate.'

'Sierra 538, we've got a fella in front of us here. There's a light gone on in a house. We're just checking the area out. Just stand by.'

The 'fella', a resident, had been woken by the commotion. He told them what he had seen.

'Sierra 538, the offenders have taken off on foot. Probably back on to Glenmere. They're on foot through a walkway [to] there.'

While the other vehicles closed in on Glenmere, Sierra 478, the Nollamara van, arrived in Adela Place to help check the vehicle with Milne and Briggs. Maybe the offenders had run off. And maybe they were watching from behind one of those darkened brick fences.

Two wide, two in close, the officers slowly approached the Cordia. Revolvers drawn and torches raised, they kept a wary eye on the houses as they checked inside.

Empty.

'Sierra 478, there's a scanner in the vehicle. There are shotgun cartridges in the vehicle and there's no shotgun we can find at the moment.'

'VKI: So they've still got the firearm, do they?'

'We presume they still have it.'

Later they would find a balaclava in the car. And the camera, with those pictures.

Milne and Briggs headed back to Glenmere and Dugdale to brief the Division 79 cars.

'We had our lovely pale blue shirts glistening in the moonlight and .38 revolvers,' Milne remembers. 'The Division 79 guys had flak jackets and shotguns.' All yours, fellas.

But before they had a chance to brief them, a phone call from a resident to police headquarters provided a lead.

'VKI: Delta 4, head for 33 Glenmere Way. Two people believed to be there that shouldn't be.'

'Delta 8, backing up.'

The armed teams crept along the street and checked the house in question. Nothing. The next day, in the next yard, they would make an unnerving discovery: impressions and scuff marks behind the brick fence.

Abbott, cool as a cucumber, had chosen to wait it out. He and Reynolds crouched there for several hours, literally holding their breath. The pendulum of luck had swung their way again. The police combed the area until 4.30 am, but concluded they had slipped the net.

For Phil Milne, a police officer for just a few months, the night would live long in his memory. What if there had been a police helicopter in Perth, back then? What if they'd known who was in the car when the chase started? What if the search had continued until daylight? But hindsight was no help.

Abbott, curse him, was just a lucky bastard.

He was also spooked. The money didn't matter any more. They had to get out of Perth. Now.

Later that morning, the pair stole two motorcycles from the Curtin University car park and hit the road. They barely paused until reaching Adelaide, almost 2500 kilometres east.

They were short on cash, but Abbott didn't want to give away their position with another job. He needed some space. Reynolds had family in Adelaide. Maybe they would be good for a loan.

He asked his grandmother in Elizabeth Park if he could stay for a few days, but she was ill and his visit didn't help her recovery. Next was his grandfather in Craigmore, who wanted to know what he was up to. Was Abbott with him?

'Yes, he's back at the place we're staying.'

'Have you got guns?'

He wouldn't answer.

In desperation, Reynolds tried an uncle in Davoren Park. But his family didn't have the sort of money a fugitive needed. There was no other choice: hit a bank and keep moving.

On December 21, the Kent Town Commonwealth Bank was robbed of $8000. A single bandit walked up to the counter, dropped a bag in front of a teller and pointed a sawn-off pump-action shotgun. 'Fill it up.' It was all over in 30 seconds.

Still on the motorcycles, Abbott and Reynolds headed to Temora, 350 kilometres south-west of Sydney, to catch up with the man named on Abbott's false driver's licence — Mark Mannion. The old boys' network was working well. The ex-con met them and arranged motel accommodation for three nights. For the first time in weeks, they were able to pause for breath. The pressure was off, at least for the moment, and the pair were able to relax for Christmas.

On December 27, they dumped the motorcycles in the Murrumbidgee River and caught a train to Sydney from Wagga Wagga. The next day it was Wollongong, and another motel for three days.

Around this time, there was a report that Abbott had been seen near Newcastle. A tip-off led to a raid on a local club, without success. Later, intelligence would indicate that Abbott paid associates to make false sightings. He never minded investing in his own safety.

Their ex-con mate reckons he left them on December 30, just as they were about to board a bus for Sydney. The next day, it was on to Adelaide. On the Canberra–Adelaide leg, Abbott struck up a conversation with a 32-year-old Japanese tourist, Masao Ayuda. He fancied himself as a bit of a linguist and it is said he took a course in Japanese while in Fremantle. 'We're engineers on holidays,' he told Ayuda. 'Walter and Peter.'

Abbott played the generous local, offering to give him the benefit of their local knowledge. Ayuda was on a package trip, with pre-booked accommodation and transport. 'We'll tag along,' Abbott told him. The accommodation and transport could be arranged as they went.

They spent New Year's Eve in Adelaide, and the amateur photographers were back in action. There's a moody shot of the Adelaide Town Hall clock, about to strike 12 on New Year's Eve, and another of the Lord Mayor's party out the front. The next day, there was a trip to a museum and some local sightseeing.

On January 2, it was back to work. Tourism, escapee style, was a costly business. At 9.45 am, a man in a blue balaclava and carrying a large blue bag walked into the Kent Town branch of the National Bank — the same one hit back on December 21. He pulled a sawn-off pump-action shotgun from the bag and pointed it at a mother and her two sons. 'You, you and you. On the floor.'

He then turned to two other male customers. 'And you too.'

He tossed the bag over the counter to a teller. 'Just keep filling it up. I don't want to hurt you, I just want the money.' She stuffed cash from a nearby trolley into the bag and passed it back, but he wanted more. He kept filling it as she passed more money on to the counter.

He turned and walked out at a brisk pace, heading straight to a waiting red Commodore, firmly grasping the bag containing $19 000.

The timing of the robbery was no accident: Ayuda was scheduled to leave on a bus that day, bound for Uluru (Ayers Rock). They took some photographs at the bus terminal, Abbott

an aerial shot of the Croc Hotel in Jabiru. Back in Darwin, there was a visit to the crocodile farm at feeding time. Not that Abbott and Reynolds were hard to impress, judging from the dozens of photos.

After Fremantle Prison, drinking a bourbon in a hotel pool and raiding the mini-bar rated pretty high on the excitement scale.

By January 9, Ayuda, and possibly Abbott, had moved on to the Acacia Court Motel in Cairns. But whether Reynolds was still with them by then is doubtful. Abbott had devised some post-holiday plans which didn't include his fellow escapee. It was simple: he was of no further use to Abbott. It was time to split up.

Ayuda, meanwhile, finished his holiday, returning to Tokyo on January 19 with pleasant memories of his time in Australia. But they turned sour when the International Investigations section of the Tokyo Police came knocking on his door later that year. They wanted to talk about the second Kent Town robbery and his travelling companions. He didn't.

The inspector who conducted the interview reported: 'After some persuasion, he agreed to come to the interview on October 2, while saying that he had no direct knowledge of the robbery and the memory had started to fade away. If possible he wished to forget about this matter.'

Ayuda offered scant details of the trip, but did mention that his companions were 'fairly heavy drinkers'. And they had insisted he always drive the hire cars they used. We don't have licences, 'Walter' and 'Peter' told him.

After the trio split up, there had been no further contact. Ayuda returned home. Abbott had business to attend to. Aaron Reynolds headed back to Perth. But his business was strictly personal.

He may have been grinning in the photos, but inside, Reynolds was a cauldron of emotion. The Top End tour had sidetracked him from his original reason for escape. In April that year, he had married his girlfriend in prison and was looking forward to starting over when released. They had secured a Homeswest house in Bunbury, south of Perth, and Reynolds was granted a transfer from Fremantle to the regional prison.

Then it all started to go wrong: his wife changed her mind just before the transfer went through. She stayed in Perth, while he was left to sit in a Bunbury jail cell and ponder what had gone wrong. There was only one option: he would escape and find out.

After cutting a hole in an outer fence, Reynolds returned to Perth and contacted his wife. She convinced him to give himself up but, in his mind, things were only getting worse. She wasn't going back to him, and Reynolds felt that an extra six months for the escape plus a return to Fremantle was harsh. Then, as his lawyer later explained, 'By tragic coincidence, he met another man who was [his] co-offender. He has an awesome criminal

fell under this man's influence.' And so it went.

Now, Reynolds was back. He wanted to sort things out with his wife once and for all. But staying out of trouble without Abbott was no easy task. At about 7 am on January 11 he was sighted near a shopping centre in north suburban Balga. But despite a two-hour search by dozens of police, he slipped through the net.

When *The West Australian* reporter Helen Winterton interviewed a friend Reynolds had been visiting in the area, he warned her: 'He's a violent bastard and all the media coverage could make him mad. The media should just stay out of it, because there are a lot of people he could hurt if he gets angry. He seemed OK when he came over. I mean, how would you feel if you had every cop in Australia after you?'

Pretty desperate, it seemed. The next day, Reynolds went to a Westpac branch in Osborne Park with Craig Atkinson, another ex-resident of Fremantle. Reynolds went in wearing overalls, a hat and a mask, armed with a 12-gauge shotgun. But bank robbery methodology wasn't his forte. Instead of singling out a staff member, he ordered them all to the ground. No one reacted when he demanded money. It's just not the sort of job that encourages volunteers.

Reynolds pumped the 12-gauge's action and remodelled a desk in the rear of the bank office. Still no one moved. He lost his nerve and bolted. Atkinson drove them to a nearby bowling alley and they later slipped away.

But the Armed Robbery Squad was still working overtime. Detective Sergeant Garry Annetts met an informant later that day who told them Reynolds and Atkinson were at a house in

Rivervale, but they weren't staying long. The detectives and Division 79 officers stormed the house that night. Reynolds and Atkinson were both sleeping and barely had a chance to react.

As Garry Annetts charged into a bedroom, Reynolds rolled off the bed towards his weapon, but thought better of it and surrendered. But he wasn't about to accept defeat with good grace. During the series of court appearances that followed, he threw a chair at a media artist and tore a telephone from a wall. There was even a suicide attempt, after the enormity of his situation had sunk in. But he survived, going on to serve almost nine years' hard time.

Holidays with Brenden Abbott, it seemed, came at a high price.

Chapter 6

Dangerous shadows

'I feel like I am the only person in the country who does not think of Brenden Abbott as a hero. I despise him, and I think I have a right to.'
— Adelaide bank robbery victim

The man in the overalls didn't look like a bank robber. At least not at first glance, as he crashed to the floor, back turned to the staff.

'Oh, the poor cleaner,' someone cried and rushed over to help. He climbed from his knees and turned, the balaclava and long-barrelled pistol stopping the Good Samaritan in her tracks.

'This is a hold-up. Put all the money in the bag. Don't do anything silly or I'll shoot.' He walked forward and placed a bag in one of the teller booths, the security camera capturing the terror of the moment. A single, cowering hand, just visible above the counter; the solid, menacing bandit standing above, pistol waving.

The bag was soon filled, but he seemed in no hurry. The shrill sound of a hold-up alert on police frequencies was difficult to miss, and the scanner in his overalls, connected to an earpiece, was reassuringly quiet. There was still time to check the place out.

He had seen another staff member walk into the strongroom and set the treasury timer to unlock. He followed her in. 'Open it.'

'It's on a timer.'

'How long's it going to take?'

She answered and he paused, appearing to think it over. It was too long. The $25 000 in the bag would do for now. He strode to the door, pausing to issue a parting shot. 'Next time, I'll shoot.'

The robbery — on the Westpac branch in Woodville Park on 26 January 1990 — marked the start of a major headache for Adelaide detectives. Over the next 24 months, there would be 12 more robberies involving about $503 000. Eventually, the list of suspected Abbott robberies in South Australia would reach 18.

It took time to connect them, though — there was no Armed Robbery Squad in the southern capital, and a new detective was assigned from the relevant suburban branch as each robbery occurred. Each time, they would return from a scene and run the details past the Bureau of Criminal Intelligence (BCI): 'Got anyone who fits this?'

Each time, they would get the same answer: 'Yeah, WA reckon it could be a bloke they're looking for. Brenden James Abbott.'

Not that they seriously believed he did them all. In fact, any detective in any city who suggested Abbott as a robbery suspect would always refer to their 'open-minded' attitude to the investigation in the same breath. Of course they did: Commonsense dictated that a single man couldn't have robbed a bank every two months for two years.

a single bandit targeting the big money, to a group of men using a car as a front door key and robbing the tellers.

But for all the evidence pointing to a wider group of offenders, the detectives couldn't help coming back to the picture painted by the subtle details: the lateral thinking, the bandit's speech, the developing sophistication, the intelligence gathering, the bags, the type of gun, the jokes. And on many occasions, the entry before or after trading hours.

Perhaps Abbott's peers had been taking notes. Maybe he had expanded his operation. Either way, he wasn't the sort of man to put his hand up to a bank robbery, even if they could track him down. And there was never enough evidence for charges.

Only the men in the masks would ever know the truth.

The Woodville Park bandit, it seemed, was a man of his word.

On 25 May 1990, a man in a balaclava walked into the busy Westpac branch, pushed an elderly woman aside and casually announced: 'Don't worry, this is just a hold-up.' He placed a black sports bag on the counter and ordered the teller to fill it.

Other staff began stacking money on the counter, but one was too slow for the robber's liking. 'Hurry up, I haven't got all fuckin' day.' He pumped the shotgun's action and the teller hastily complied.

A phone began to ring. 'You'd better answer that. It'll be your security ringing.' No one moved. He walked along the booths, sweeping the money into the bag, and headed for the door with $26 000.

'Have a nice day. I don't have to work any more.'

Whatever his professional activities early that year, Brenden Abbott was certainly relaxed enough with his situation to re-establish a cautious personal life. He met a young blonde woman in Coolangatta, on the Gold Coast, and struck up a casual relationship.

Louise Laycock knew him as Peter Holden, a nice, if somewhat mysterious bloke, who would stay with her for short periods and then vanish without explanation. Just a few months after they met, she fell pregnant, and in December that year gave birth to Abbott's son, James Leslie, in a Blacktown hospital.

He made a point of ringing Laycock on the boy's birthday and at Christmas, but maintaining contact with any family members was inherently dangerous, given the likelihood of police surveillance. He also rang his mother regularly after the heat died down, but eventually stopped, fearing her phone was bugged. He was right. The emergence of pagers and mobile phones provided Abbott with new communications options, although he was careful not to become complacent. He would regularly replace communications equipment and identities, minimising the chance of police phone intercepts.

As well as finding time for fatherhood, Abbott indulged his love of cricket and cars. Glenn Abbott let slip that his brother spent at least one summer in the early 1990s enjoying international cricket games around the nation. And there always seemed to be a car project on the go. He liked and used Toyota LandCruisers, and he had a passion for adding horsepower to restored Holdens.

But there wasn't time for much else. Staying on the run was a 24-hour-a-day job and a low profile was important. His average-looking face had an almost chameleon quality, depending on which particular identity he was using at the time. A pair of glasses, short curly hair, shaved head, moustache, goatee, beard, rapid weight gain or loss. Depending on the combination, he could look like a completely different person. And his skills with a make-up kit complemented the package. Abbott also kept on the move, a different man with a different name to most who met him.

But despite the careful move into anonymity, the bank robberies plaguing Adelaide kept his name in the news. Among them was another drop-in job, this time at a National branch in the city, on 21 June 1990.

Two men entered the Morphett Street branch via a toilet, surprising staff just before they opened for the day. While they took care of business in the strongroom, the getaway driver was double parked outside, dealing with a determined parking inspector. He didn't have time for a ticket and indicated his displeasure with a warning shot. The inspector didn't stop to argue the point.

The trio escaped, and while they didn't grab spectacular headlines, the robbery's drop-in aspect was part of a new, wider terror in the psyche of the nation's bank staff. The method of entry was unheard of until Abbott pioneered it back in 1987. Now it was becoming a regular feature, and was giving the average bank teller a nervous disposition. Noises in the ceiling used to be written off as possums, workmen or noisy pipes. Now, they took no chances. A tense search would usually end with a terrified possum staring down the barrel of a police shotgun. Unpleasant for the possum, but necessary for the staff's peace of mind.

As well as his contribution to bank robbery methodology, the staff also became familiar with Abbott's name. Initially, it inspired fear, but in later years, his constant media exposure angered them. After Abbott's 1998 recapture in Darwin, one National Australia employee, 'Nicole', couldn't contain herself any longer. In an article published in the *Advertiser* she wrote of her experiences in two robberies, one of them a fixture on the list of suspected Abbott jobs. She also recalled a third incident: arriving at work to be confronted by Special Tactics and Rescue officers checking out a possible 'job':

A police officer took me to a relieving manager. I wanted to ask him what was happening but I just couldn't speak. The incident was taken so seriously because the modus operandi was that of Brenden James Abbott. How that name has haunted me since 1991.

The terror of the robberies had lived long and vividly in her memory, affecting every detail of her daily life.

One day, you are one person. The next day, you and the world have changed. It's a strange feeling, but from the morning after the first robbery, I knew life would never be the same. You no longer wake up without thinking about what you might encounter in your day. You think constantly of your own survival.

I have not been on any form of public transport for seven years. That is an impossible fear, not being able to control just when you can escape from a bus or train.

For a long time, I couldn't go into shopping centres, picture theatres, restaurants or anywhere people gather. You don't know who might be in these places. The anxiety is unbelievable.

At first, I could not go to sleep like a normal person. I watched TV until I was exhausted. When I closed my eyes I would see a man wearing a balaclava. I lost weight and [had] frequent panic attacks. I cannot, even now, sleep in a dark room.

I have walked in my sleep, hitting windows with my fists, screaming to get out, and calling for help. I began to live my life around the hold-ups. It seems almost every decision had something to do with them.

I got married in a garden, as the thought of being married in a church, in a building, caused too much anxiety. I shopped only where I knew I did not have to enter shopping centres. I would always ask where toilets were in any building, because of the constant fear of being sick from panic.

Mostly, I became an expert at excuses. I was so good I think I even started to believe some of them myself.

I have seen a psychologist, who helped me get this far and says my progress is good. If this is where I am after seven years, I wonder how long it will be before I feel comfortable with myself.

At the moment I feel like I am the only person in the country who does not think of Brenden Abbott as a hero. I despise him, and I think I have a right to. People seem to forget bank robbers are only a trigger away from being murderers.

In July 1990, yet another Adelaide job put Abbott back in the headlines. The Commonwealth Branch at the West Lakes

Shopping Centre was robbed of $55 000, two men smashing their way through a door with a rifle just before opening time. Detectives announced Abbott and an unknown accomplice as the suspects, and suggested he was using scanners to stay one step ahead. Years later, advances in technology would add credence to their theory. An old piece of forensic evidence, unidentifiable at the time, pointed in a single direction — but it still wasn't strong enough for a charge.

And the robberies just kept coming. On 2 November 1990, a bandit smashed his way into the Modbury branch of the Westpac Bank, five minutes after the staff had locked the doors for the day. Wearing a balaclava, gloves, khaki overalls and armed with a shotgun, he strode over to the banking chamber's doorway. 'Give me your fuckin' cash, and hurry up!' The staff froze.

'Do you think I'm fucking joking? Move!'

The tellers began filling the black sports bag he had placed on a table. He walked over to the ATM room and tried the door. 'You think I'm messing around, but I'm not. I know there's someone in there. Get the key and open the door or I'll blow a hole through the cunt.'

A teller walked over, knocked on the door and it was reluctantly opened. 'Come on, open them and give me the money,' he told the woman inside. But the ATM cartridges were still in the machine.

He found the staff with the combinations and waited outside the room while they gained access, but precious minutes had passed. A green van parked at the front door started to beep its horn. Time to go. He grabbed the bag from the table and sprinted for the door with $14 000.

always measure success. On-the-job training could bring longer-term rewards.

Someone had been doing their homework: $160 000 for five minutes' work. It was 25 January 1991, another year and another bank robbery in Adelaide.

Two balaclava-clad bandits in unnaturally bulky overalls — a feature of many of the suspected Abbott robberies — smashed their way through a rear door at 5.10 pm. The first bandit, with sawn-off shotgun and sports bag, jumped the counter and headed straight for the strongroom. The second, larger bandit stood at the counter and watched the staff, backs turned and arms raised.

Sawn-off shifted his attention to the ATM, putting his bag and gun on the ground and attempting to pull a cartridge out. 'Open it for me,' he told the nearby staff member.

She unhooked the $50 and $10 cartridges and lifted them out. He grabbed them and returned to the main banking chamber, where semi-automatic was at a teller's box checking for cash.

'And the other one.'

'There's nothing in there,' the teller replied.

'Don't mess with me.'

He peered over to check and she pulled the empty cash drawers open to prove it.

Sawn-off stopped to finish filling his bag, then headed for the door, fully laden with cartridges, bag and weapon. Semi-automatic grabbed his takings and followed, walking backwards and keeping his weapon on the staff. They opened a rear door and left, the staff waiting expectantly for its alarm to trigger. It remained silent.

Three weeks later, the Western Australian Police updated their Most Wanted list. 'A convicted armed robber who has committed violent robberies in nearly every state while on the run for more than a year is WA's most wanted criminal,' *The West Australian* reported.

'. . . The 28-year-old has fired shots at police and reportedly sleeps with his favourite firearm, a sawn-off pump-action shotgun.'

The intrigue was growing, and not only in Western Australia.

Detective Senior Constable Trevor Jenkins received a startling introduction to the Abbott investigation in July 1991. Stationed at Elizabeth CIB, he'd lived and worked in Adelaide's far northern suburbs for the best part of 30 years. But he'd never seen anything quite like the robbery on the Salisbury Commonwealth Bank branch on the afternoon of July 19.

'People just don't drive cars into banks,' he says, still incredulous seven years later. 'There wasn't even any need to do it. They could have got in with a hammer.'

At 5.15 pm, a Ford Laser screeched from a laneway in reverse, jumped onto a footpath and crashed into the bank. There were two bandits in the car, but Jenkins suspects there was a third keeping watch, giving them the signal to back out of the blind laneway.

The car crashed through the window and came to rest a few metres from the teller booths, the front still protruding onto the footpath. While the passenger hit the teller booths, the larger bandit, armed with an unusual military assault weapon, kept watch.

As $32 000 was placed in the passenger's khaki bag, an elderly man peered through the shattered shopfront to ask if everyone was

patrol entered from the other side.

The near-miss sent a chill down Jenkins' spine. 'If they had been 20 seconds earlier, they would be dead,' he says of the officers involved. He had no doubt the men involved in the Salisbury robberies would shoot, and their heavy duty armory and MO indicated there was more to come. Abbott remained his best suspect, and he soon found himself filling the gap as the South Australian link in the wider investigation.

Late in November 1991, Glenn Abbott applied for — and received — an Australian passport while still in prison. When Thelma Salmon collected it from her son during a visit, Jeff Beaman fired off a memo to Jenkins, warning that Brenden might use it to leave the country or as a means to get other forms of ID. Beaman described the brothers as 'almost twins', and a video of the pair together, taken during the Fremantle Prison riot trial, backed up his assertion.

A camera was on hand for the regular strip searches of the prisoners before court, and it captured the brothers handcuffed together on several occasions. Glenn was sullen, a belligerent 20-year-old who was wary of the camera and kept his head buried in his chest. In contrast, his larger brother appeared alert, glancing around as the other prisoners and guards bustled about. He chatted easily with the guards and on one occasion, waves his appendage at the camera with a wry grin. But with both brothers sporting a full head of dark, curly hair, and each with tattoos on their upper left arms, the similarities were unmistakable.

It was probably fortunate that Glenn was still in jail. The last thing the detectives needed was look-alike brothers robbing banks. A defence lawyer would have a field day with the identification issue in court.

And as to the suspected accomplices in the Adelaide robberies . . . no one's talking. The detectives say they have their theories, but over the years, intelligence on Abbott associates became a key part of the overall investigation. And intelligence, by its very nature, requires secrecy.

The third and final Salisbury robbery, on 20 January 1992, involved a single bandit in the bank. The car stayed outside this time, with a waiting accomplice. But from the moment the bandit tried to lower himself from the ceiling at 8.50 am, it was a dog's breakfast. A staff member investigating noises in the ATM room found him dangling from the ceiling, caught up in cabling. He was in overalls and looked like a workman, but a glimpse of the balaclava had her reaching for the nearest alarm button.

Once free, the bandit went out and grabbed two staff members and ordered them to remove the ATM cartridges. As he watched them struggle with their task, his nervousness grew. He knew the

wasting time. You're wasting my time. Get them out.'

An agonising two minutes later, one of the cartridges pulled clear. 'Is there much in there?'

'I doubt it, it's just after the weekend.'

Only $400. His timing could have been better. And now the sirens could only be a matter of minutes away. He fled the bank, but two civic-minded couriers gave chase as he and the accomplice drove off. They couldn't shake them, and after arriving at a car park to pick up the second vehicle, one robber — no doubt the one having the bad day — sent a couple of shots in their direction. The couriers took the hint. The bandits escaped, probably to ponder the fickle nature of bank robbery's most important element — luck.

Trevor Jenkins, on the other hand, thought his might finally be changing. In the previous two years — on 26 January 1990 and 25 January 1991 — there had been bank jobs timed to hit the cash reserves on hand for the Australia Day long weekend. The latest robbery was on the Monday before the long weekend. Perhaps the robbers were trying to mix things up a little by striking earlier than expected. If so, their gamble had failed. It was fair to assume that they were now angry and still in need of cash. Would they roll the dice on the Friday and hit the long weekend reserves? Jenkins wasn't prepared to chance it. When Friday afternoon rolled around, he was ready.

Throughout the Salisbury area, detectives were hidden in banks and credit union branches. Each had an open line radio, minimising the response time for the STAR Division officers and police helicopter on standby. As closing time approached and passed, the tension mounted. But the bandits made no move.

Jenkins switched to Plan B. The STAR Division officers were shown the cell block video and sent to the Adelaide Oval for the weekend. If Brenden Abbott was in town, there was every chance he would be sipping a cold one under the scoreboard at the Australia Day Test Match. But there was no sign of him.

There would be no more suspected Abbott robberies on the suburban detective's patch, and the entire file eventually passed back to the Organised Crime Task Force, which had first compiled the list.

Investigating Brenden Abbott left its mark on Jenkins. Seven years later, he recalled the details of each robbery as if they had occurred last week. But like so many detectives, it wasn't Abbott's public image which drew him to the case. Rather, it was his firm belief that it could only be a matter of time before someone was killed. His final word: 'There is no single criminal that concerns police — and should concern the community — as much as Brenden Abbott.'

Chapter 7

Golden opportunity

'How much is there, mate? Six hundred, seven hundred thousand? I'm going to have a good Christmas.'
— Brenden Abbott to bank manager
during Queensland's biggest bank robbery

The Western Australian Armed Robbery Squad hadn't forgotten about Brenden Abbott, but pursuing him was proving to be a difficult task. There were legal hurdles, with several jurisdictions involved, as well as the prohibitive costs and logistics of tracking Abbott from the other side of the country. Instead, the detectives could only act as navigators in the other states' investigations, which remained separate, despite their common goal.

During the early 1990s, investigating officers from around the nation would recognise the problem, but convincing their superiors that an armed robber required national action wasn't easy. Jeff Beaman, who had cast himself in the role of dogged Abbott pursuer, always believed it was the only way they would catch him. Abbott was a moving target, which made intelligence coordination essential. But it was, at best, piecemeal.

Beaman and his sergeant, Geoff Maloney, would often sit

patiently through phone calls from different detectives in different states asking the same questions. Sometimes, the interstate liaisons would produce useful intelligence.

Louise Laycock's name first arose after a police informant in Darwin spotted the Abbott/Reynolds holiday snaps in an *Australasian Post* article. She knew Laycock from Murwillumbah, in northern New South Wales, and recognised Abbott as Laycock's boyfriend. The Darwin detective who received the tip passed it on to the Bureau of Criminal Intelligence in Sydney. Out of courtesy, he contacted Beaman to update him on events, but to Beaman's knowledge, there was no follow-up on the tip in New South Wales.

A few months later, in July 1992, he took a call from another interstate detective. He was from Murwillumbah, and had a couple of questions about a domestic dispute involving Louise Laycock which had landed on his desk. He had rung Beaman because Abbott's name had come up and BCI had alerted him to Western Australia's interest in the case. But it was academic by then. If Abbott had been in Murwillumbah, he would have been gone at the first sign of trouble. Perhaps if the Darwin tip had been acted on immediately, they might have been on to something.

It was situations like this, Beaman says, which led to stand-up arguments with BCI officers. He was furious at the lack of communication. Some called it the Black Hole — a cynical, but half-serious jibe suggesting that while plenty of information went in to the BCI, nothing ever seemed to come out.

On one occasion, Abbott was sighted in Perth on a Friday and a report was made to a suburban CIB. It eventually reached the Armed Robbery Squad the following Monday. The details were dutifully passed on to the BCI. 'That can't be right,' they told Beaman. 'He's not here, he's in Queensland.'

'Oh really? What makes you think that?'

'Nothing specific. He just is.'

Beaman couldn't quite believe their attitude. And they didn't seem to understand that Abbott could be in three different states in any given week.

A few weeks after the sighting, his anger was vindicated. A man seen talking to Abbott at the time of the sighting was arrested in Merredin, east of Perth, on another matter. Beaman interviewed him. Yes, he'd seen Abbott. They bumped into each other in the street and said g'day. On that day, at least, it seemed he was nowhere near Queensland.

But eventually, other intelligence would lead the Western Australian detectives to believe that Abbott was using the northern state, the Gold Coast in particular, as his main base. When Beaman went to Queensland for an unrelated extradition, he tried to drum up interest among their detectives, but no one seemed enthusiastic, he says.

In hindsight, they should have been. The smell of money on the Gold Coast was palpable, and Brenden Abbott had been refining his skills in preparation. Bigger rewards would require better methods.

Getting in was easy. The night before, Abbott had tampered with the lock on the rear fire escape door, allowing him easy access late the next afternoon.

It was Thursday, 16 April 1992, and the National Australia branch at Springwood, on Brisbane's southern outskirts, had just closed for the Easter break. Abbott strode through the bank's lunch room, balaclava in place, pistol at the ready. 'Who the hell are you?' the stunned accountant asked as he emerged into the main banking chamber.

'You, you and you, out the back here.'

One teller was sent around with a bag to empty the drawers, but Abbott became agitated at her lack of haste. The nine-millimetre pistol suddenly discharged, the slug lodging in a table. 'Sorry, it wasn't supposed to go off. I should have put the safety on, shouldn't I?'

He shifted his attention to the ATM, apparently already aware of who he needed to speak to. 'Is it open?'

'No.'

'Don't give me that shit, I know you've got the key.'

The cartridges were soon being emptied into the bag, which now contained over $203 000. Abbott headed for the door.

'Thanks very much. Have a good Easter.'

'Yeah. Thanks, mate.'

It was the first of six robberies — involving $1.7 million — and one attempted robbery which would later appear on an indictment bearing Abbott's name. He would, of course, fight the charges — inch by legal inch — but there were few yawns during the protracted court battles.

The Brisbane and Gold Coast officers did their homework and, for the first time, hard facts would give credence to Abbott's image as a cold, calculating, career criminal. At times, incredulous judges would interrupt to check they had heard correctly.

In the end, after exhausting every legal option, Abbott was found guilty by a jury of one robbery. Then, after a judge ruled that five of the other six charges could be heard together, Abbott finally agreed to a plea bargain: guilty on two counts, remaining charges dropped. Even he wasn't prepared to risk a trial this time around.

The Gold Coast and Brisbane detectives had prepared similar fact evidence that was as meticulous as it was overwhelming. And while Reilly was careful to point out that 'it was not the same method on each occasion. It became, progressively, far more sophisticated', the similarities were unmistakable.

The robberies, he said:

- Were committed outside bank trading hours, but while staff were present.
- Involved a heavily-built bandit wearing a dark balaclava, reflective sunglasses or both, carrying a handgun.
- On some occasions, involved a second, smaller

bandit, but the larger bandit always appeared to be in charge.

- Involved the use of a sports bag to transport the proceeds.
- Involved entry through a staff door, usually at the rear.

'Threats were made after a surprise entry which had the effect of overwhelming any ideas of resistance by the bank staff,' Reilly told Judge Boulton during a defence application for separate trials in March 1997.

'The heavily built bandit was, in many instances, talkative, asking questions, telling of his knowledge of the premises and of procedures, and in some instances wishing the staff a happy Easter or happy Christmas. In five of the six robberies [Abbott had already been convicted on the other count] the door had been drilled in such a way that the lock could be manipulated in order to gain entry. There is evidence linking Abbott to a storage shed at Burleigh Heads, where police found drilling equipment. In five of the six robberies, the robber used or understood bank terminology, in particular the use of the word treasury. In three of the six robberies there was interference with alarms which would have required sophisticated understanding of their operation and would have required the person responsible to have gained prior entry to the bank in order to carry it out.'

In some instances, he said, a lock was altered from the inside. In three of the six robberies, the bandit had a scanner and focused on the ATMs, netting large sums from their cartridges. In three, possibly four, of the robberies, there was evidence that the bandit bought a getaway vehicle for cash shortly before the robberies and then abandoned it nearby.

a clear signature, and one in particular showcased Abbott's skills like no other before it. Detectives later described it as his *pièce de résistance*. In one, he was strategist, intelligence analyst, electrician, locksmith, communications expert, make-up artist and, above all, violent felon.

The target was the Commonwealth Bank branch in the Pacific Fair Shopping Centre, at Broadbeach, on the Gold Coast. At the time, detectives marvelled at its audacity, and even now — with the benefit of all the details — no one's quite sure how it succeeded.

And the bottom line, as Bernard Reilly would later tell a court, carried its own weight: 'It was an amount, on my instructions, which remains the largest single amount of money obtained from any bank in a robbery of this type in Queensland.'

So how did Abbott — and at least two accomplices — walk away with \$781 252 on Friday, 24 December 1993?

Sitting in the shade of some bushes next to the bank, headphones in place, Brenden Abbott scanned the surroundings. It was still early. Soon the Pacific Fair Shopping Centre would be filled with crowds of last-minute Christmas shoppers. He watched as a bank

<table>
<tr><td colspan="2" style="text-align:center">

VICTORIA
AUSTRALIA
REGISTRATION OF BIRTHS, DEATHS AND MARRIAGES REGULATIONS - FORM 2

BIRTH CERTIFICATE

</td></tr>
</table>

1 CHILD	
Family Name	**ABBOTT**
Christian or Given Name(s)	**Brenden James**
Sex	**Male**
Date of Birth	**08 May 1962**
Place of Birth	**Footscray**

A section of Abbott's birth certificate, showing one of three variations in the spelling of his christian name — Brenden, Brendan and Brendon.

COURTESY *The West Australian*

Abbott, sitting in the door of a police van, waiting for a court appearance in Perth in 1987.

Homemade prison guard caps used by Abbott, Aaron Reynolds and another inmate during the escape from Fremantle Prison in 1989.

Aaron Reynolds grins for Abbott outside the Dwellingup police station, in WA's south west, while on the run in 1989.

Abbott and Masao Ayuda at an Adelaide bus terminal in January, 1990.

Abbott and Aaron Reynolds at the South Australian Museum of Natural History in January, 1990.

The mini-bar facilities met with Abbott and Reynolds' approval during their luxury 'holiday' across Australia.

'People just don't drive cars into banks' — Detective Sergeant Trevor Jenkins. Two bandits rush to a getaway car at the Commonwealth Bank in Salisbury, Adelaide, in July, 1991, during a suspected Abbott robbery.

Two bandits smashed their way into the Campbelltown Commonwealth Bank on 25 January, 1991, escaping with $160 000 taken from ATM cartridges and teller drawers.

'Don't do anything silly or I'll shoot.'
A bandit controls the banking chamber at the Woodville Westpac branch in Adelaide, 26 January, 1990. Police suspect Abbott was the offender.

This entry in a Fremantle Prison visitor's book for tourists was written while Abbott was on the run, following his escape from the prison in 1989. Handwriting tests were conducted, but nothing was conclusive.

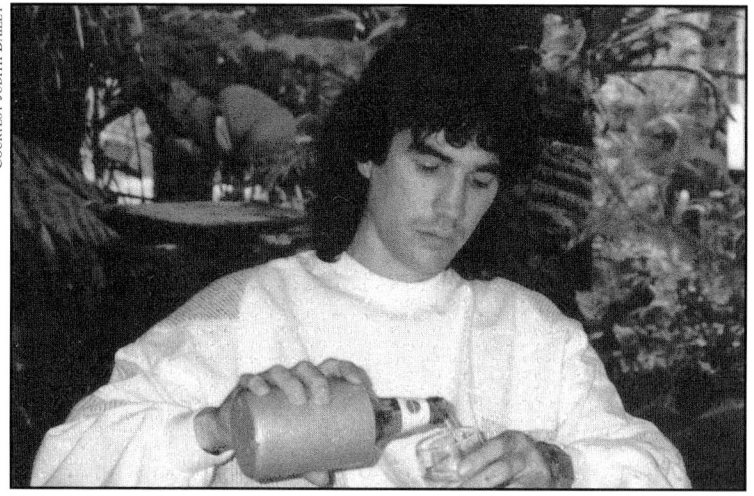

Abbott associate Trevor Bailey regularly provided him with a safe house at his family's home in Launceston, Tasmania. Bailey vanished in January, 1993.

A picture of Abbott found in a Tweed Heads storage shed used by his girlfriend. It gave a rare glimpse of his appearance in the early 1990s, and was the first picture in which Abbott was clearly identifiable to Queensland bank robbery victims.

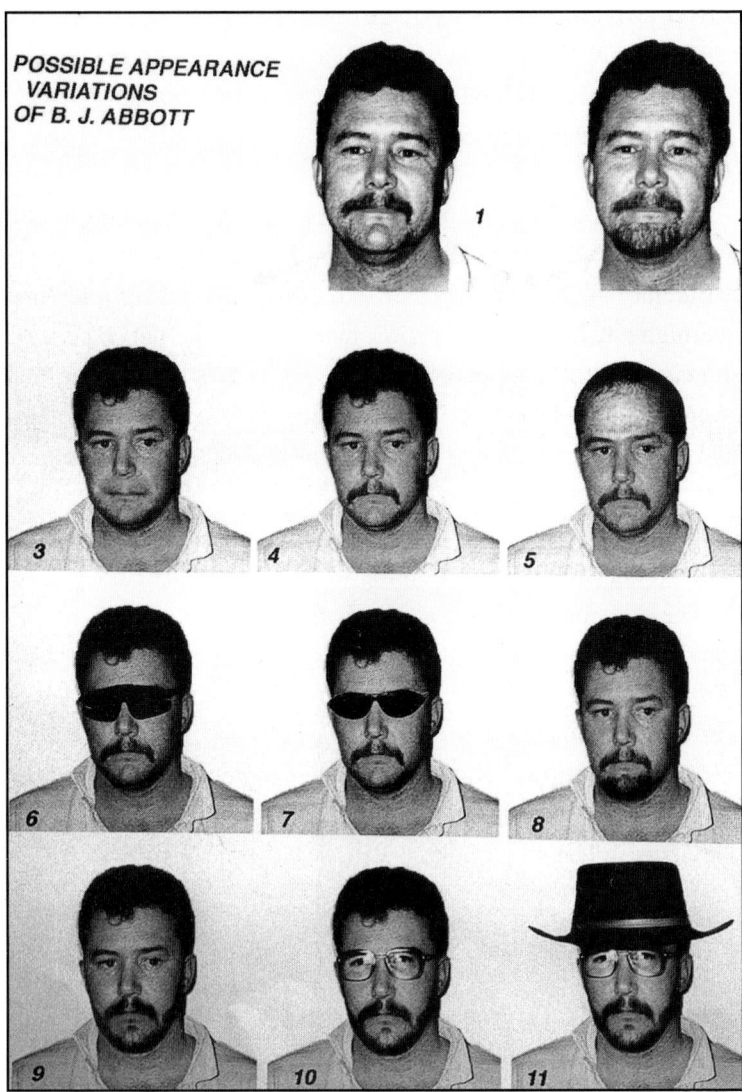

POSSIBLE APPEARANCE
VARIATIONS
OF B. J. ABBOTT

A police photoboard shows possible variations of Abbott's appearance.
He was often described as a master of disguise: he was handy with a make-up
kit and his fluctuating weight also helped alter his facial appearance.

officer arriving for work walked towards where he sat near the rear fire exit. She was suspicious, and watched his reaction as she commented, 'It looks like it's going to be a hot day.'

'I just wanted to get cool, love.'

Hmmm.

She walked forward and shook the fire exit, checking that it was locked. Abbott held his breath. The door — the lock, in particular — had undergone extensive internal remodelling overnight. It had a lever action handle with a 'locked' sticker showing on the inside. But fiddling with the mechanism and swapping the stickers had solved that problem. The size of the screw holes on the door's inside chain had also been increased, with the screws wedged gently back into place with glue. It looked secure, but would only require a solid nudge to dislodge the single screw helping to hold it in place.

The door held. Abbott exhaled. But the bank officer wasn't convinced. After completing further external security checks, she told her colleagues to keep an eye on the man in the headphones while she completed the internal procedures.

Everything appeared to be in order. No one in the building, doors locked, ceiling panels in place, alarms tested and operational. The staff trickled in, and preparations for the day's business began.

An amount of $100 000 was removed from the treasury and distributed to the tellers, in anticipation of the last-minute Christmas rush. There was plenty more where that came from, but Abbott still had one hurdle to clear before he could access it safely. Using the rear fire exit was only viable if the alarm could be disabled — if it activated, he wouldn't have enough time to target the treasury.

Problem: If disabled, it would be discovered during the morning security check.

Solution: An internal remote switch fitted to the door's alarm box.

It still operated when the alarms were tested, but just before Abbott and his accomplice crashed through, he activated the remote switch, cutting a crucial wire in the system. How? No one's sure. The locks on the alarm box had been changed as well and, before leaving, Abbott used his key to gain access and remove evidence of his handiwork.

Just on 9 am, Abbott, in cap and sunglasses, and his smaller accomplice, with false beard and sunglasses, burst through the fire exit. Abbott ordered the staff to sit near the strongroom, but several remained standing, defiant. Suddenly, he became agitated, complaining that he had lost his radio transceiver. 'Did you see where I dropped it?'

No one replied, but his threats and the pistol finally prompted a teller to point it out on the floor. He reconnected it to his earpiece. 'All clear?'

'All clear,' the reply crackled back.

Outside, a passer-by paused to ask the man in the suit for the time. But he was simultaneously keeping watch, listening to a scanner and updating his accomplices via a two-way. No, he didn't have the time.

'Fuck off, pal.'

By now Abbott had calmed down, reassured that he was still in contact with his look-out. But bandit number two remained twitchy, standing in front of the teller boxes, nervously rubbing his elbow, weapon pointed at the floor.

'Don't even think about using the alarms,' Abbott told the staff.

'We've got a scanner and we'll know the instant the police are called. I'll kill someone if an alarm goes off.'

He turned to the manager. 'Where are the others?'

'I don't know what you mean.'

'Come on, where are the others? Don't fuck me around.'

'They're over at [another branch].'

'What about the short fat one with the cream top?'

'She's just gone to Coles to get some morning tea for the staff.'

'What about the treasury? What sort of timer is on it?'

No answer. Abbott cocked his pistol and pushed the barrel into the manager's chest. 'If you don't fucking tell me, I'll waste you.'

The moment slowed, stretching as the manager's fate hung in the balance. Abbott then lowered the tension, adopting a more tactful approach. 'You're the manager, the staff will do what you tell them.'

A phone rang, and the manager turned to answer it.

'That's a good idea.' Abbott leaned forward to listen in, making sure the caller wasn't tipped off.

Bandit number two, meanwhile, was asleep on the job. Abbott turned to scold him. 'Don't turn your back on them! Never turn your fucking back on them.'

He turned back to the manager, who somehow managed to complete the call to Abbott's satisfaction. 'Who's got the keys for the treasury? And I want all the fuckin' teller keys.'

The keyholders identified themselves and one of the staff who had remained standing began collecting the teller keys. She considered reaching for an alarm button if the opportunity arose, but couldn't bring herself to do it. There was no doubt in her mind it would cost a life.

Abbott watched her face telegraph the thoughts. 'Jeez love, I thought you'd blown it for me,' he told her as she and the manager were directed into the treasury.

He noticed the manager studying him closely. 'I know what you're doing, mate, you're trying to look at me. Don't bother, I'll give you a description.'

After the time lock released on the treasury, Abbott leaned in to survey the bundles of cash. 'How much is there, mate? Six hundred, seven hundred thousand? I'm going to have a good Christmas.'

'We won't,' the manager replied.

'You'll get over it.'

But he didn't.

Three days later the manager would disappear, his family and colleagues dreading the outcome. He turned up 36 hours later in a motel room, with no idea how or why he had gone there. And he wasn't the only one to be haunted. Of the 12 staff present that day, eight left the bank, and of the remaining four, one took long-term stress leave.

As the manager began stacking the money into the large sports bag, Abbott reflected on the rewards of careful planning. 'I know this place. I know it like the back of my hand,' he told them. He grabbed the bag and ordered all the staff to a tea room upstairs.

The manager crept down several times to check to see if they had gone. On one occasion, he saw them fiddling with the alarm box and heard several further situation reports on the radio from the suited accomplice. But no one saw them leave and no getaway car was sighted.

Triumphant, they vanished.

Bank robbers had become something of a pest on the coast, and the Gold Coast Armed Robbery Squad was formed in June 1993 to deal with the problem. It seemed a sensible and obvious move, but it actually went against the grain of modern police investigative methods. The unending revelations of corruption through the late 1980s and early 1990s had led to inevitable changes in Australian police culture. In most states — and most had a corruption scandal at one time or another — it was the detectives who came in for the most attention.

Senior police believed the tight-knit culture of the CIB squads was a fertile breeding ground for corruption. Their static nature, and rarely changing line-up of detectives, meant they sometimes got to know the villains — and each other — too well. As a result, many squads were cast to the four winds as each state pursued its own solution to the problem.

Specialisation became an anachronism, as suburban CIBs swelled in size and the detectives, now expected to be instant experts, moved from robbery to assault to arson. Wider investigations were assembled from scratch, the detectives moving on when they were completed. But phrases such as 'proactive policing' and the 'efficient, focused use of resources' still seem to leave the average detective cold. Familiarity may have its failings, but many still believe it is the key to criminal investigation.

Detective Senior Constable Glen Prichard, one of four detectives attached to the Gold Coast Armed Robbery Squad, arrived at the Pacific Fair bank minutes after Abbott and his accomplice had disappeared. The case would be his, although Abbott's name

taken the trouble to change the genuine tattoo on his upper left arm from a seahorse to an Indian's head.

Drill holes found in the front door locks several days after the robbery solved the mystery of how they had gained entry. Prichard estimated that the bandits had spent at least 30 minutes inside the bank setting up.

Detective Senior Sergeant Gerry Costello, from the Brisbane Armed Robbery Squad, had shown a photoboard of the Abbott 'postcards' to victims of previous robberies, without success. This time, they had another picture with a more current likeness, seized from a Tweed Heads storage shed used by Louise Laycock. It had been taken shortly after the birth of James in Sydney in 1991 and showed a smiling Abbott with his son. Seven

Pacific Fair staff pointed it out. As Prichard put it, 'It looked like we were on the right track.'

After Prichard compared the robbery to earlier suspected Abbott jobs, he began searching the *Gold Coast Bulletin* for clues. The getaway cars seemed to be bought from newspaper ads shortly before the robbery and then dumped, but this time leads were harder to find. After pouring over the classifieds and contacting the sellers, Prichard hit paydirt: a man who had advertised a 'reliable' Sigma picked Abbott from the photoboard. He had sold the car to him for $2400, cash, on December 19, five days before the robbery.

The car finally turned up in October the following year when a check of vehicle records revealed it had been re-registered by a local council worker. He had bought the car from a German man, Hardy Brasche, who was a known Abbott associate. When questioned, Brasche said he sold the car in early January 1994, on behalf of a man he knew as 'Pedro' Holden. He only got $1200 for it, but Pedro, Brasche said, made sure he collected the money. Abbott might have pulled the state's biggest bank robbery a few weeks before, but business was business.

The detectives took a close look at Brasche, hoping he would lead them to Abbott. He was one of many Queensland associates who would be placed under surveillance, but without success. And while there were more sightings of Abbott in the months after the robbery, there was still nothing solid. But Abbott had gotten away with too much for too long — and far too easily. The ever-increasing number of detectives investigating him were tired of chasing shadows. Sooner, rather than later, they would come after him.

The vanishing

'I think I could cope knowing he is dead. It's terrible, but living like this is even worse. It's a nightmare you never wake up from.'

— Judy Bailey, mother of missing Brenden Abbott associate, Trevor Wayne Bailey

He loved the place, but the Gold Coast wasn't Brenden Abbott's only regular haunt of the early 1990s. After his escape from Fremantle Prison in 1989, regular movement around the nation became a key to his continued success as a fugitive. And depending on the city, he could usually find a bed with an old mate. In prison, many young men fell under his spell and were more than happy to help his cause. After their release, they could provide valuable extra options when he needed them most.

This theory is backed up by an Australian Bureau of Criminal Intelligence report. It identified a loosely organised group of ex-cons, known simply as The Network, who would aid prison fugitives. Trevor Wayne Bailey, an excitable, hyperactive young Tasmanian, was among them. Bailey had arrived in Perth in 1986 from Launceston, where he had already had several brushes with the law. A few months after his arrival, Bailey, then 19, went berserk. There were house breaks, seven stolen cars and, in a ram raid spree, at least four breaks on liquor stores and supermarkets.

After being arrested, he and his accomplice bashed a police officer who was taking them to court. He was out of control. But Abbott — who met him in Fremantle in 1987 while on remand for the Belmont job — recognised potential. And after Bailey was released in July 1991 and returned to the family home in Launceston, it didn't take long for the phone calls to start.

A few months later — in about November — Abbott began making regular trips to the Bailey household. Pete, he called himself. A solid, imposing man with short curly hair and glasses. According to Trevor's mother, Judy, he was a laid-back bloke who rarely swore, didn't touch drugs or alcohol, and enjoyed a laugh. 'He never used to throw money around. You never saw him running around with thousands of dollars in his wallet.'

Cooking breakfast in her home one morning, he dropped and broke a toaster in the kitchen. 'Mum'll bloody kill you when she sees that,' Trevor warned him. She couldn't help but laugh when 'Pete' went straight out and bought her a new one.

And when Trevor broke his leg in a traffic accident, 'Pete' rushed straight over from the mainland to see his mate in hospital. He flirted with the nurses and 'certainly had the gift of the gab', Mrs Bailey says.

Nothing seemed out of the ordinary. He was a mate of Trevor's who was enjoying taking a break in Launceston. Not that he went out much. Watching videos seemed to be his favourite pastime. But later, Bailey would show his mother the 'postcards' article published in *Australasian Post*. 'Don't cross this bloke, mum. This is who he is,' he warned her.

how they could get by on what they earned between them. Trevor seemed happy.'

But he was also careful, telling his mother that if Abbott called, she wasn't to mention Laycock's presence. Laycock stayed about a week and then returned to the mainland after an enjoyable but seemingly uneventful trip.

Abbott was back again before New Year's Eve, a few days after another robbery in Queensland with which he would later be charged. This time, it was on Christmas Eve, at the Coolangatta branch of the Commonwealth Bank. But the charge would be among those dropped in the plea bargain.

Abbott stayed at the Bailey home a few days into the New Year. He had brought a younger, dark-haired lad with him. Judy Bailey didn't mind playing the cordial host, but she was getting a little tired of running a hotel for Trevor's friends.

The young man stayed only the one night at her home, and on January 2, Trevor drove the pair to the airport. He followed five days later, his father dropping him off at the terminal. He didn't say where he was going, but Judy Bailey got the impression it was to join Laycock in Queensland.

The next night, there was a brief phone call. 'Mum, as soon as I get to where I'm going, I'll give you a call,' Trevor told her.

'OK, mate. Take care.'

She has never seen or spoken to her son since. A week later, Louise Laycock rang. 'Is Trevor there?' she asked.

'No, I thought he was up your way,' Mrs Bailey replied.

'Well, he was here on Sunday night when I went to bed. When I got up Monday morning he was gone and all his stuff was still here.'

Mrs Bailey was mystified, but not particularly worried. Trevor travelled a lot, and this wasn't unusual. They'd hear from him soon enough: even when in prison, he would always write or call.

Laycock promised to give Mrs Bailey a call when she found out were Trevor was. She never did.

'It was probably 12 months or so before I reported him missing,' Mrs Bailey says. 'I knew something was wrong and had wanted to do it sooner. If he could, he would have reversed the charges. We haven't got much, but if our kids needed help or a plane ticket home, they knew it was there for them.'

In the end, she couldn't wait for the phone to ring any longer, but it wasn't an easy decision. Balanced against the fears for her son's safety was the risk that police involvement could land him in deep trouble — if, in fact, he was still alive and mixed up in something serious. She went ahead and made the statement, outlining her knowledge of Trevor's movements before he disappeared.

Later, a story about *Abbott* on the *Today Show* would stop her in her tracks. She'd seen that face before. The report was from Adelaide. She was soon on the phone to Sid Thomas, a detective sergeant at Darlington CIB who was pursuing Abbott over a robbery at a Glenelg bank in July 1994.

The involvement of Abbott in the case led Thomas to take an interest in Bailey's disappearance, and he checked possible leads in Adelaide and Perth. There really wasn't a lot to go on, but he thought some publicity for the case may help uncover fresh information.

Later, in 1995, the author would float one of the detective's theories on Trevor Bailey's fate in an article headed: 'Love rivalry link in bank bandit saga.'

'Police suspect a bitter love triangle involving Australia's most notorious bank robber, Brenden James Abbott, may have ended in murder,' the article said. It had the desired effect of flushing out fresh information on the case, but none of the new leads developed into anything tangible.

But whether or not the salacious allegation was true is another story. When Glen Prichard later questioned Abbott about Bailey, Abbott laughed it off. And Sid Thomas would also put it to him, explaining the anguish Mrs Bailey felt at not knowing whether her son was alive or dead. But if he knew, he wasn't saying, and Thomas carefully recorded Abbott's exact response in his notebook. 'Are you looking for him? . . . I don't think he's around.'

The detective also travelled to Western Australia during his inquiry into Abbott, and took the time to visit Glenn Abbott in prison. But after the formalities were completed and he mentioned Bailey's name, 'the conversation never really got off the ground'.

'He became aggressive and that was basically the end of it,' Thomas says. Not that aggression from Glenn Abbott could be construed as guilt. He was, after all, a man who would later shoot a police officer rather than accept a speeding fine.

So what really happened to Trevor Bailey? 'I believe he's dead,' Mrs Bailey says with sad conviction. 'I believe he was probably murdered, but I don't know who by. Trevor may have been in the wrong place at the wrong time or may have opened his mouth at the wrong time.'

Sid Thomas and, in particular, Rob King, from Launceston CIB, made every effort to find her son, she says. But Mrs Bailey is more frank about the situation than the diplomatic detectives. 'Whatever Rob has tried to do, he's not got any help from the mainland police,' she says. 'He was always the last to know anything. When [Abbott] escaped, you would think they would contact the Tasmanian Police. Sid Thomas is very understanding, too, but no one else seems to care except when Brenden's on the run. No one seems to give a damn about Trevor.'

Judy Bailey flicks through a collection of family photos, reflecting on the suffering her family has endured. 'Trevor was basically a good person, a good son. Now, I don't think I have any sons.' His brother was killed in a car accident in 1990, the day before his 21st birthday. The continuing mystery of her other son's disappearance adds to the weight on her mind.

'I think I could cope knowing he is dead. It's terrible, but living like this is even worse. It's a nightmare you never wake up from.'

Trevor Bailey is thin with a slim build. He usually had long, dark, wavy hair. He is 178 centimetres tall, with blues eyes, olive complexion and has a small scar on one cheek from a tattoo removal. On 2 March 1999, he would have been 32 years old.

Chapter 9

Changing tactics

'Congratulations on year five. Regards, Freddie and Myrtle.'

— Message on Brenden Abbott's pager,
23 November 1994

Everything fitted but the date. The robbery at the Modbury National Bank in Adelaide bore all the traits of an Abbott operation. The language, level of planning, physical description, and a conversation between the bank manager and the bandit all pointed in his direction.

But it was 30 December 1993, just six days after the Pacific Fair robbery in Queensland. Was Abbott really that desperate for money? It seemed unlikely. And this was just one of many instances in which police intelligence would place him at opposite ends of the country around the same time.

Abbott has always complained, with some justification, that the police seemed to want to pin every unsolved robbery in the nation on him. An exact figure is difficult to calculate, but his name came up in at least 70 armed robbery investigations around the nation in the first half of the 1990s.

However, there was no police conspiracy to focus on Abbott. For much of the time, they simply weren't telling each other what was going on, at least on an official, coordinated level. And well-planned, unsolved bank robberies are not an everyday occurrence in Australia. The list of suspects is either short or non-existent. With each state relying on the police grapevine to pass on intelligence and Abbott's reputation continuing to grow, it was inevitable that his name would usually top such a list. But it doesn't explain the Abbott trademarks in the Adelaide robbery — and a host of other unsolved robberies in South Australia, Victoria and New South Wales.

Was Brenden Abbott part of a larger, organised group of criminals, using similar methods and planning? Or — as his defence would later suggest in regard to the Queensland robberies — were the skills involved the sort of thing any bright young criminal could pick up?

The Modbury bank manager pulled to a stop in the rear car park at 8.20 am. He paused before getting out, his curiosity aroused by the strangely dressed man walking towards him. He was wearing a black curly wig with a ponytail sticking out from underneath, khaki-coloured shirt and pants, new blue canvas shoes and wool gloves. Later the description would be more detailed: thirties, white, dark brown eyes, clean-shaven, big face, about 185 centimetres, with a thick build and a 'flabby stomach'.

'Good morning, I've got an appointment here,' he called out cheerfully.

'Oh, yes.'

The manager began gathering his possessions from the car when the 'client', who was also carrying a blue bag, walked over and squatted down next to the open driver's side door. He took a pistol from his pocket and began to speak calmly and clearly.

'Just remain seated. I've got some instructions for you. I'm here to rob you. Get out of the car and do everything I ask.'

The manager climbed out and they began walking slowly to the back door of the bank. 'I'll be taking you hostage after the event. I'll keep you for two hours and then I'll release you, assuming everything has gone smoothly. You'll recognise my face and you'll be giving a description of me to the police, but you're not to identify me in an identification parade, because I've got the registration number of your car. And you'll notice that I've got my sleeves down so you can't see my tattoos.'

He might have looked like an escaped mental patient, but there was no doubt that all lobes were working. They reached the door. 'I want you to do your entry procedure as you normally would.'

The manager pulled his keys from his pockets and began to fumble with the lock.

'How much would you have in there?'

'I don't know.'

The bandit persisted, eager to find out if he had picked the right moment. 'How much did you have in there yesterday?'

'A couple of hundred.'

'How much is in the ATM?'

'I don't know. It depends on the usage.'

'What's an average figure?'

He then asked for the names of all the staff members. Calling victims by their first names may have seemed a friendly gesture, but bank employees would beg to differ: it scared them on a deeper, lasting level.

'I've been watching you for a week, there's [sic] six of you,' he said, as he placed a white mouth and nose cover, similar to a surgical mask, on his face.

At 8.30 am the manager met one of the staff at the door when he heard his key scrape in the lock. 'Take it easy, Peter,' he told the young man. Peter looked at the bandit.

'Put your things down and lie face down. I'm going to tie you up.'

He did as he was told, and his ankles and wrists were bound with silver tape.

'Who's got the other combination?

'Either Joanne or Stacey,' the manager answered.

'So we're waiting for either Joanne or Stacey.' He looked out the window expectantly. 'Someone else is coming.'

The manager and bandit went through the same procedure with the next unsuspecting employee arriving for work. She was tied up and carried into the stationery room. The bandit returned to drag Peter in as well. He then returned to the window, out of breath and sweating from the effort, but he would have to repeat the process three more times.

Finally, Joanne arrived. It would take several minutes to deal with the remaining security procedures before the bandit stood in front of the coveted treasury. He looked questioningly at the manager.

'It's on a time delay,' he told him.

'How long have we got?'

'Six minutes.'

He spoke into the walkie talkie again: 'We have to wait six minutes.'

The manager wanted it over. Every extra minute increased the chance of someone getting hurt. 'The phones are going to ring soon,' he warned his captor.

'Answer them as you see fit.'

Another staff member arrived while they were waiting for the time lock and he soon joined his bound and gagged colleagues. Just as a bell announced the lock's release, a phone rang. Someone from the Currie Street branch wanted to talk to Peter. 'Can you call back later? He's busy at the moment,' the manager told the caller. He returned to the strongroom and opened the safe.

'You put the money in,' the bandit told him. From the blue bag, he produced a large green canvas bag, similar to the type used by armoured guards. Thirty seconds later, he was stuffing the filled bag back in, with the manager's reluctant assistance. 'You've done very well. I'm going to tie you up.'

Trussed up and lying face down, he waited to hear the rear door close before stumbling into the stationery room. His shocked but relieved staff looked up from the floor.

'Everything's all right. He's gone.'

Abbott's life seems to have continued idyllically through the early part of 1994. He was content on the Gold Coast, which was now his favoured base.

The problem was, he was too comfortable. On May 27, he made a fateful decision to establish a link to the outside world, renting a box at the Mermaid Beach Post Office. The mobile phones and pagers had proved a handy form of communication, but even fugitive bank robbers have to pay their bills — and they had to be delivered somewhere.

And brother Glenn was definitely back in the picture by now. He was proudly running his own little support operation back in Western Australia. Large parcels were regularly crossing the Nullarbor in both directions.

Of course, Abbott used all the usual precautions, using a false identity to rent the box and no doubt checking the area thoroughly before approaching to open it. But later, it was a decision he would regret.

The day after he rented the box, Queensland Police updated their Most Wanted list. Abbott was on it, of course, but surprisingly, despite all his suspected robberies, the detectives still hadn't issued a warrant for his arrest. It probably seemed the least of their worries. First, they had to catch him.

The following month, a new woman entered Abbott's life. He was in Cairns when he met Georgia Smith, a 'masseuse' in her mid-twenties who was working at a local establishment. Later, like so many others, she would claim not to have known his true identity. She only knew him as Barry, she would tell police, a nice guy who said he worked in the hotel industry.

Abbott returned to visit her several times, and although he only stayed at her home once, Smith thought she was on to a good thing. Money seemed no object with Abbott, and she joined him on two trips to Melbourne and one to Darwin, all expenses paid. It also seemed that the fugitive wanted some domesticity in his life, a rare luxury while on the run. Later in the year, he asked Smith to move to the Gold Coast and live with him. She agreed.

But before then, and unknown to him, Abbott's situation underwent a major change. It began, naturally enough, with a bank robbery.

On Friday, 22 July 1994, a bandit lay in wait on the roof of the Commonwealth Bank branch in Glenelg, a coastal Adelaide suburb. At 8.15 am, an unknown accomplice gave him the signal via a two-way radio, just as the first staff members arrived for the day. He smashed through an upstairs wall and hid in a toilet, then confronted two staff members as they stopped off in the lunch room. He took control of the banking chamber, and told the staff to continue letting their colleagues in as usual or he would kill someone.

During the 30-minute robbery, the bandit sat at a desk and put his feet up. There was no need to worry: he had a microphone on his collar and was in constant contact with his accomplice.

Brisbane and Gold Coast Armed Robbery Squads were both actively hunting Abbott, and there were also detectives in Victoria and New South Wales who were monitoring his activities. So it was no coincidence when the Western Australian, Queensland and South Australian detectives all fired off memos to their superiors within a few weeks of the Glenelg robbery. One submission read:

> *Abbott has been aptly described as one of Australia's most notorious criminals, even if only a small proportion of the offences he is attributed with*

having committed have in fact been committed by him.

He has shown considerable planning and organisation, a secure network of criminal associates, extreme daring and a blatant disregard for the lives of his victims and police.

The investigation into the Jetty Rd robbery highlighted difficulties confronting investigators in South Australia and agencies around the nation, including inadequate intelligence, despite the number of robberies he is suspected of committing.

Detectives investigating the Jetty Rd robbery made inquiries with agencies in other States. This demonstrated that there was in fact a considerable amount of information known by individual agencies, but not much available to the investigators.

His robberies are always extremely well planned and executed and invariably involve lengthy surveillance on the target premises. His criminal network is extremely secure. A considerable number of persons, predominately bank staff, have been victims of his crimes over the past five years.

He is considered armed and highly dangerous. The potential for a fatal shooting of a bank employee or customer is very high.

The detectives recommended the formation of a national task force, with experienced Abbott investigators gathering in Adelaide for a conference. They also wanted a central agency to coordinate the distribution and collation of intelligence, and an increase in the paltry $10 000 reward on Abbott's head.

The conference never eventuated, but the Australian Bankers Association increased the reward to $50 000 and the detectives got their task force — Probe: Flanders. The Australian Bureau of Criminal Intelligence became the hub of the investigation, ensuring that all the detectives were kept up to date on developments in the other states.

At last, the hunt had begun in earnest.

Glen Potter was faced with a daunting sight when he transferred from Division 79 to the Armed Robbery Squad. Geoff Maloney and Jeff Beaman had moved on, and a room full of boxes bore testament to the squad's lengthy pursuit of Abbott. But after trawling through the mountain of paperwork, Potter came to the obvious conclusion that the trail, at least in Western Australia, had gone cold. Abbott was obviously based elsewhere, and local associates and informants were proving to be of little use. They suspected Abbott had been in contact with his mother through a third party, but none of the family were volunteering any knowledge of his whereabouts.

'No, Sergeant, we haven't heard from him. We don't know what's going on.'

Potter also concluded that Abbott was very mobile. After speaking with Sid Thomas and Lou Major from the Brisbane Armed Robbery Squad, he showed similar enthusiasm for a joint approach. And Potter already had ideas for his contribution to the investigation.

While most of the family members had been easily tracked down, Glenn Abbott seemed to have vanished. His last known address, after his release from prison, was with his mother.

He was now calling himself Glenn Salmon, a name taken from his mother's short-lived second marriage to John Salmon.

At one point they thought they'd found him, but after a surveillance operation was set up, it turned out there were actually two Glenn Norman Salmons in Western Australia, of similar description and age. The man they were watching was the wrong one.

But Potter wasn't prepared to give up, due mainly to a chance piece of intelligence: Glenn's de facto wife, Kelly Fisher, had previously crossed Potter's path while he was in Division 79. She had contacted police after an ex-boyfriend, also a criminal, had threatened to kill her. Potter checked out the report and, in the course of his inquiries, spoke to Fisher's parents. Kelly had told her mother that Glenn had disappeared for three weeks. She was expecting to come into a lot of money as a result.

At the time, the information was irrelevant to Potter's investigation, but it now held special significance — the three-week period coincided with the Pacific Fair robbery. And it seemed that Glenn was now going to great lengths to keep a low profile. That was enough for Potter: Glenn Abbott had to be found.

In fact, on 2 November 1994 — the day the Western Australian detectives met with BCI analysts for the first time to discuss strategies for Flanders — Glenn Abbott was on his way back to Perth. Evidence recovered later showed that he had stayed at the Pink Poodle Motel on the Gold Coast from October 30 until November 1. He used the alias Barry Reid, paid cash and gave a fictional address in Alice Springs.

Some time early on October 30, a large amount of ammunition and rifles had been stolen from Gold Coast Shooters Supplies in Ashmore. And it was no smash and grab raid.

detectives involved in Flanders. Of course, Potter gave no hint of the current operation, but he confirmed that Abbott was still being sought and that the reward had been increased to $50 000.

Around the same time, Glenn Abbott's driving skills gave him the break he needed. He was pulled over for a traffic offence and gave his real name. When the officer checked his details via the police radio, it set the alarm bells ringing. On November 17, when Glenn faced a Mandurah court over the traffic offence, they were ready for him.

The surveillance team swung into action, and over the next three and a half months they would help to build a picture of

Glenn's carefully concealed life. He was living with Kelly Fisher at a house in Halls Head, near Mandurah, an hour's drive south of Perth. The house rental agreement, electricity, telephone and vehicles parked in the driveway were all under false names. They checked his mail and found he was using a post office box in Rockingham, a coastal town between Mandurah and Perth. There were regular deliveries to the box of anti-personnel sprays and electronic surveillance equipment from American mail order companies.

Around this time there was a report of a sighting of Brenden in Mandurah, and Lou Major came over from Queensland to further his inquiries. But Glenn had been regularly altering his appearance, and as Jeff Beaman had previously pointed out, the brothers could look like twins when they put their minds to it.

At one point during the operation, a curious call to Crime Stoppers asked for the name and number of the officer in charge of the Abbott investigation to be broadcast on Perth radio station PMFM's Morning Crew. Potter made the appropriate arrangements with the station's general manager and the message was broadcast. A single call came through to the number. The caller hung up immediately.

Potter believes it may have been Abbott, or one of his inner circle, checking to see who they were up against. Later, Abbott would indicate that he always took an interest in who his pursuers were and what they were up to.

Glenn Abbott was also trying to stay one step ahead of the game. He was well versed in anti-surveillance techniques and led the BCI surveillance officers — 'the dogs' — on a merry chase. On one particular day, he drove down a dead end road in scrubland at Baldivis, near Rockingham. It appeared to be a drop-

Advertiser (Adelaide). And it seems they were well-received.

'Read financial papers yesterday. Had the largest article regarding your company ever written. Congratulations, Greg. Send you a copy soon,' read the message on Abbott's pager on November 20.

And then, on November 23: 'Congratulations on year five. Regards, Freddie and Myrtle.'

The publicity also sparked several new leads, with unfortunate consequences for one of Abbott's peers. On November 24, an Adelaide taxi driver became suspicious of a man who was flashing cash and said he was from Western Australia. It wasn't Abbott, but when detectives arrested the man at a Glenunga motel, they were at least half right. He was on bail for armed robbery in Western Australia and was wanted for questioning over another one. He was soon on a plane back to Perth.

Brenden Abbott, meanwhile, was busy setting up permanent lodgings on the Gold Coast. His offer to Georgia Smith was too good to refuse, and after staying at the Pink Poodle Motel for several days, they moved into Unit 54, Florida Apartments, on the Gold Coast Highway. Abbott came and went, but it became Smith's permanent residence. He paid the rent and household bills, and she had a car and a generous monthly allowance. He even paid a $4000 plastic surgery bill after she had her nose and breasts touched up.

On December 4, a pager message to Abbott indicated that some money was being shuffled around. 'Have been to post box. Received cheques. Waiting to know when to clear. Michael.'

The paging service would be kept busy over the next couple of months. So would Brenden Abbott.

A million things can go wrong in an armed robbery. And sometimes, they do.

Case in question: a staff member arrives for work early on 16 December 1994 at the Westpac Bank, Broadbeach, on the Gold Coast. The prospective bandit was just finishing up his preparations in the bank when the dedicated employee arrived at 7.30 am. Via a two-way radio, he indicated to his unknown accomplice waiting outside that things were definitely not going to plan. He tried to salvage the situation, but waiting several hours for the key staff members to arrive was out of the question. He threatened the man and demanded money, but it was useless. The bandit left in a hurry, leaving a scanner behind. Abbott would later be charged with the attempted robbery, but it would be dropped in the subsequent plea bargain.

He appears to have remained on the Gold Coast through the summer, and the pager messages continued thick and fast:

his work, in the midst of the intense and public investigation.

The precision of the robbery at the Pines Shopping Centre, at Eleanora on the Gold Coast, was such that detectives initially estimated that it involved up to three months' planning. But Abbott had it down to a fine art by now. It was probably more like a couple of weeks. The doors and alarms had been taken care of the previous night, and he lay in wait in a back room. (But he made what would prove to be a crucial mistake, somehow cutting himself and leaving a blood smear on a wall.)

He stepped into the doorway at exactly 8.47 am on 20 January 1994 wearing regulation balaclava, microphone and gloves, waving what appeared to be a semi-automatic pistol. 'I want you all over here,' he indicated with a wave of the pistol towards the hallway behind him. Abbott removed a scanner from a large blue sports bag, which he then thrust at one of the staff.

'You look the calmest. You do it.'

He began screwing an aerial on to the scanner. 'You know what this is, don't you?'

'I know what you mean,' the staff member replied, understanding that if the alarm was raised, it would soon be broadcast on a police frequency.

He ordered the staff about, clearing the obstacles of the alarms and locks on the ATM. After $354 000 was transferred to the sports bag, he said: 'I want you to turn the cameras off.'

'There are no cameras running.'

Just to be sure, he made them explain the exact camera procedures. Extra intelligence always came in handy.

'Right, I want youse all in this room.' The staff shuffled obediently into the interview room. 'Stay here until my ride gets here, shut the door.'

'I'm still here,' he called out twice, before they finally heard the front door buzzer. He stepped past a teller arriving for work, and was gone.

Detective Senior Sergeant John Ponting, of the Gold Coast CIB, told the *Courier-Mail* that Abbott was the prime suspect. 'The offender was extremely organised and was cool and calm throughout the robbery,' Sergeant Ponting said. 'Before leaving the bank, he removed his balaclava and walked through the car park wearing wraparound sunglasses and a baseball cap.'

Abbott and an accomplice fled in a yellow Cortina which was found less than 100 metres away in an underground car park. Sergeant Ponting said that the robber possessed 'an intricate knowledge of the workings of the bank. He knew exactly how many staff members worked there and the exact procedure of the bank staff and security.'

bandit's precision. The judge who later sentenced him for the robbery described it as a 'well planned and professionally executed robbery'.

At least one of his associates agreed: 'Congratulations on business transaction. Fred.' read the message on Abbott's pager three days after the robbery.

The same day, Glenn let his brother know he was on his way over to help celebrate. 'Halfway there. Will contact you soon. Michael.' The next day, they met up at a hotel in Cairns.

Later that month, the Queensland detectives decided that the media publicity was getting out of hand. Phrases such as 'the nineties Ned Kelly', 'larrikin criminal' and 'Postcard Bandit' didn't sit well with them. 'Make no mistake, this bloke's dangerous,' they told the *Courier-Mail*. But in their efforts to quash the myth, they instead added some more cloth to the tapestry.

'Right now he could be sitting back with his favourite drink [bourbon] and watching the Test Match [his favourite game is cricket] right here on the Gold Coast,' an unnamed 'senior detective' was reported as saying. 'But he'd likely be doing it in some moderately priced unit — not one of the flashy expensive joints, and he'd be eating a fried chicken takeaway — not eating at some five-star joint.'

It was right on the mark, and was the sort of comment that endeared him to the public as much as the Postcard Bandit myth ever did.

But the suburban hero was about to be brought back to earth: Glenn Potter had settled on some new tactics for his investigation. The results would not easily be forgotten.

Chapter 10

Betrayal

*'Correction. The old man stinks. Your post office box
stinks and Fat Boy stinks. Regards, Dirty Girl.'*
— Last message received on Brenden Abbott's pager,
10 am, Friday, 10 March 1995

It may have been just before 7 am, but Senior Constable Graham
Randall had good reason to be cheerful when he strolled into work
on Tuesday, 7 March 1995. It was his birthday and he was looking
forward to celebrating with his family that night. And he had no
complaints about the work. Being a member of Division 79, the
Western Australian CIB's Rapid Response Unit, was a prized
position in the eyes of any young constable with a thirst for action.

But more importantly than the job, life itself was good.
Randall was happily married, and the arrival of his daughter just
over a year before had changed his life. It had got him thinking.

Division 79 was high risk. Being a front-line officer
investigating the city's most serious crimes wasn't compatible
with raising a young family. It was time to move on.

But instead of heading for the relative safety of the suburbs, he
was pursuing a different option — the Canine Section. The idea

face was a loaded single-barrelled shotgun. On the other end was an angry man.

'Drop the gun, drop the gun!' Randall shouted. The man ducked back into the shadows and Randall's finger tightened on his own trigger — just as he heard the other weapon clatter to the floor.

No, this wasn't a situation a doting father should consider engaging in on a regular basis. But he was happy to bide his time in Division 79 until his transfer came through. After last week, the odds were he'd stay out of trouble until he left.

And today, the odds were even better. The bulk of the section operated in the afternoon, evening and early morning. Real trouble prefers the cover of darkness. The day shift was far less likely to involve dangerous situations — on most days, only one car was rostered on. In fact, the only thing to disturb Graham Randall's sense of contentment that morning was the fact that his regular partner was away for several days. But that was hardly a problem. He was teamed up with Doug Nelson, a keen young detective constable who would later end up in the Armed Robbery Squad on yet another Brenden Abbott investigation.

The pair met up for the day soon after Randall arrived for work. From the start, the day was different. 'Go and see Glen Potter at Armed Robbers. He's got a job for you,' their boss told them. A job. That afternoon, they would be calling it a dog's breakfast, at least until they heard the full story.

He considered installing listening devices in his home, but Western Australia's laws at the time weren't conducive. What about cars, Potter thought. 'Why don't we put listening and tracking devices on his car?' Perfect. Especially for those romantic bushland rendezvous Glenn was so fond of. Problem was, it wasn't like the movies. There would be no men in black creeping into Glenn's garage at 3 am to clamp tiny metallic devices to his car. It took considerably more time and skill.

There was even a test run on a VH Commodore, the same make and model as Glenn's car. It was a station wagon, but a touch quicker than the average family version. Glenn took pride in the vehicle, particularly its motor's capabilities. It appeared that a skilled mechanic with a lot of time and money on his hands had been at work under the bonnet. (Coincidentally, the car matched the description of the one given by Judy Bailey, when asked about the car Brenden had used when visiting her Launceston home.)

In the end, it was Glenn's Toyota LandCruiser which proved the best option for the surveillance devices. But how could they get hold of it for long enough without raising suspicion?

went to court over the traffic offence, he did more than give away his position — he lost his licence.

The plan had already formed in Potter's mind. Glenn, typical criminal, was still driving. Let's pull him over when he's driving the Cruiser, lock him up for driving without a licence, fit the devices and give it back when he's released. As long as he could be convinced that it was an innocent traffic stop, it would work.

Enter Graham Randall and Doug Nelson. 'Hit the road but stay in touch,' Potter told them. 'The dogs are on Glenn. We'll let you know when.'

'No problem,' they answered. 'Is he a hard or soft target?'

Potter paused. Glenn Abbott had form, certainly. And given the right circumstances, he was violent. But if he believed it was a genuine traffic stop, why would he want to cause trouble? He seemed dedicated to his brother's cause and unlikely to jeopardise it unnecessarily.

'Be careful,' Potter told them. 'Just be careful.'

The call came early that afternoon. Glenn was in his LandCruiser, driving down Orrong Road, Rivervale, a few kilometres from the city — home territory for the Abbott brothers. Driving an unmarked patrol car, Nelson and Randall approached from behind. Suddenly, Abbott pulled into a driveway, jumped from the vehicle and walked straight back towards the road. Classic counter-surveillance.

Maybe he saw them, maybe he didn't. The operation continued. He soon left and they picked him up a few minutes later, still on Orrong Road, this time in Cloverdale. He veered across three lanes of traffic and turned into Wright Street. Randall and Nelson were straight on him. No point waiting any longer. He pulled over about 50 metres down the street, outside a primary school.

Randall slipped into his polite traffic cop persona and approached the vehicle. 'Interesting manoeuvre at the lights, sir. Could I see your driver's licence please?'

Abbott was polite, cooperative, casually dressed in a T-shirt and baggy shorts. 'No worries. Here you go.'

Barry Reid, from the Northern Territory.

'Oh shit,' Randall thought. 'This wasn't supposed to happen.'

'Got any other identification with you, sir?'

'Sure.'

Doug Nelson would later sum up the situation succinctly: 'Plan A was shot to shit.'

'Hang on,' Randall told Abbott, 'we just need to check this out.'

Nelson walked back to the patrol car, pretending to check the licence details. Instead, he got straight on the phone to Glen Potter. The false ID didn't seem right.

'He's up to something,' Potter thought. 'Maybe he's going to see Brenden. Better to let him go and see what happens.'

But back at the four-wheel drive, it was becoming obvious that couldn't happen. Graham Randall had walked around the vehicle, peering inside. He pointed to a smashed window. 'No, it's not stolen,' Abbott told him. 'Look, the keys are in the ignition.'

They walked back around to check. On the floor of the driver's side was a .22 casing. It was too late now. Abbott knew Randall had seen the casing. If the officer didn't react, he would get suspicious. 'There's ammunition in the car. Is it yours?'

'No. It must be my mate's. It's his car.'

silencer. They look pretty similar, don't they? You're under arrest,' Randall told him.

'Do I have to go with you?'

'Yes.'

'So I'm under arrest?'

'Yes.'

But Glenn Abbott wasn't going anywhere. Not if he could help it. A proper search of the vehicle would reveal a lot more than a silencer and a .22 casing. That meant jail, humiliation and, worse, an end to the criminal partnership with his brother. Escape, on the other hand, offered the chance of glory, headlines and, more importantly, respect from his brother.

It was no contest. In fact, he may have made the decision even before he stepped from the LandCruiser, pocketing a small canister of tear gas.

Randall and Nelson moved in cautiously, fully aware of the potential for violence at the moment of arrest. It was now or never.

Abbott slipped a hand from his shorts and swung his arm in a wide arc. The first blast hit Graham Randall directly in the eyes, blinding him instantly. The canister continued on its journey, spraying Doug Nelson in the face and reducing his eyesight to a blur. The second swipe hit Randall in the mouth, the third across his face and ears.

Randall was no stranger to anti-personnel sprays. But this was unlike anything he had felt. This wasn't a diluted spray but a deadly serious, highly concentrated CS gas imported from America, the type favoured by para-military organisations. Red-hot needles prodded his eyes, and searing heat choked his throat and lungs. Doug Nelson had fared better. But not much.

Abbott was in the box seat. Now all he had to do was make it to the LandCruiser and he was home free. But blind or not, the two officers weren't about to give up. Randall lunged forward, grabbing Abbott in a bear hug which sent them crashing to the ground. With his partner underneath the suspect, Nelson attacked from behind.

No problem, thought the BCI officer watching the proceedings from further down the road. The guys in the Delta car were well-built and fit. This bloke had no chance. But he hadn't seen the spray. And he didn't see Abbott reaching for Randall's hip.

'He's going for the gun! Grab his arms!' Randall shouted to his partner. But he couldn't get hold of Abbott's writhing limbs. Abbott fumbled around, unclipping the holster. Calling on his prison training, he slipped his little finger into the trigger guard and pulled the gun clear.

A reverse draw, perfectly executed.

'Gun, gun! He's got the gun!' Randall, lungs on fire, warned his partner. But by this time, Abbott was in control, holding Randall in a headlock. He shoved the barrel of the gun into the officer's chest, violently enough to leave a wound. Randall could feel fingers scrabbling against his stomach, searching for the trigger.

'You're dead, you cunt,' Abbott hissed in his ear. Randall believed it. This lunatic was going to spray his chest across a footpath outside a primary school — with his own gun, no less — and there was nothing he could do about it.

Images of his daughter flashed through his mind. He couldn't bear the thought of her growing up without a father. No, he wasn't going to let this madman kill him. Not with his own gun. Not without a fight.

Doug Nelson, meanwhile, had been desperately trying to pin Abbott's arms without success. He knew this was life or death and briefly considered putting a round into Abbott, but decided against it. It would go straight through and hit Graham. And they were outside a school. It wasn't an option.

He finally got Abbott in a headlock and pulled back, simultaneously choking him and pulling him clear from his partner. Randall pushed the weapon from his chest and it dropped to the ground. He reached around blindly, grabbing it and throwing it clear. It struck the school's chain link fence a few metres away. Not far enough.

A curious passer-by chose this moment to intervene. 'Do you guys need a hand?' he asked.

'Yep, get the gun, get rid of it!' came the reply.

Bemused, the man gingerly picked up the gun, walked down the road and placed it on the ground. Abbott was still struggling, but his chance had passed. The Good Samaritan helped slip the cuffs in place. 'Just sit on him, mate. If he plays around, job him,' Randall told him.

'All right, you've got me. Stop,' Abbott finally conceded. Randall struggled over to the patrol car and radioed for assistance. The cavalry soon arrived.

Later, Doug Nelson spoke to Glen Potter on the phone. Potter was laughing, unaware of what had transpired. 'I said to grab him, I didn't say start a fight,' he chuckled. Nelson filled him in and the line went silent.

Oh, fuck.

That night, Graham Randall had good reason to end his birthday at the bottom of a bourbon bottle. He and Nelson, on oxygen and swathed in bandages, had been rushed to Royal Perth Hospital after the attack. It took more than an hour before their raw eyes began to swing back into focus.

Randall suffered burns to his throat, face and ears. His lungs finally cleared up eight days later. His birthday celebration was a wash-out.

Glen Potter, also supposed to be celebrating his birthday that day, probably considered doing the same. But there was still hope. His intention had always been to put the screws on Abbott in an interview room and search his house. It was just happening a little sooner than he had expected.

The detectives were careful to keep their distance after Abbott's arrest. No point in completely tipping their hand — let him think it was a traffic stop gone wrong. A proper search of the LandCruiser was the first priority. Underneath both sun visors were two .22 pistols — loaded, fitted with silencers, safety off. Thank Christ Abbott hadn't stuck one of those in his pocket.

And there was his pager. A message arrived explaining that a postal order for $4000 was about to be sent from West Court, in Cairns, to Cloverdale in Perth, in the name of Barry Reid. Potter or anyone could be lurking in his home, including his brother. It took a full briefing with an assistant commissioner, but Potter's request for the Tactical Response Group (TRG) was approved.

Armed to the teeth, they executed a search of the home. Inside was Brenden James Abbott — the two-month-old version — and his furious mother, Kelly Fisher. Unfazed by the men in black, she hurled abuse at Potter and expressed her devotion to both brothers.

'You'll never get my man,' she told him. 'He's smarter than you. They're professionals. You guys are amateurs.'

Potter knew what she was like, but even he was bemused. 'She was as hard as nails. You would expect someone to be fairly shaken up when the TRG comes through their door, but not Kelly,' he says.

But she was only a minor distraction. The detectives were more interested in the full-blown criminal operation they had uncovered. Scattered around the house was ammunition, another semi-automatic .22 pistol, 11 .22 silencers, electronic lock picks, pepper sprays, listening devices, night vision equipment, an 18-inch silencer for a sniper's rifle and a home-made rocket launcher capable of firing incendiary devices up to 150 metres. Glenn, it seemed, had been an industrious lad.

Then there was the 120 000 volt taser — a souped-up cattle

prod with a nasty kick. 'I like to test things before I use them,' he told the detectives later. 'The taser put me on the ground for an hour,' he admitted sheepishly.

On one wall in the house was a life-size Western Australian driver's licence, minus picture. Stand in front, smile for the camera, laminate carefully and you're on the road.

On a computer they found other false documents, including a Western Australian Police ID, more Western Australian driver's licences, and birth certificates from the Northern Territory, Queensland, New South Wales and South Australia. There were also listening devices and covert video equipment secreted around the house.

Then there was Glenn's library. He was a reader of heavy duty right-wing American magazines such as *Soldier of Fortune*, a good place to find mail order companies specialising in anti-social publications such as *Home Workshop Silencers I*, *Silencers for Hand Firearms*, *How to Make Disposable Silencers Vol II*, *Principles of Improvised Explosive Devices*, *Home-Built Claymore Mines . . .*

Was this guy from Ulster or Australia?

And it seemed someone had been reading too many Chopper Read books. There were photos of a baby — in nappies, no less — holding an AK–47 assault rifle and a large pistol, and plenty of shots of Glenn showing off his hardware. Glenn's personal favourites, though, were probably from a holiday with his brother, grinning together in the snow, Brenden with his ski mask pulled down over his face.

But while Glenn's house yielded an impressive haul, it still didn't give any clues as to Brenden Abbott's whereabouts. Potter wasn't worried. He still had Glenn's pager.

The latest message read: 'Now in Brisbane. Due to catch a flight to Melbourne very soon. Please phone urgently. William.' The Victorian Armed Robbery Squad descended on the airport. They missed him, or he never arrived.

But we're getting close now, Potter thought. This isn't over yet.

The next day, Brenden Abbott was probably already on his way to Perth, unnerved at the thought of his erratic brother in a police interview room. The pager message from one of his Perth contacts the previous night said as much: 'Haven't contacted the young fellow as of yet. Will get in touch as soon as I speak to him. Sam.'

Abbott knew his brother was loyal. But he also knew his unpredictable side. If there were going to be problems, he wanted to be there to sort them out.

Glenn, meanwhile, was behind bars, cursing his luck. Why did this have to happen, just when he was settling down with Kelly and young Brenden? And what was his brother going to say? He'd fucked up and he knew it. What could he do now?

Over at the Armed Robbery Squad offices, Potter and Detective Senior Constable Steve Drown were devising an answer to that question. The next day, Glenn would step into one of their claustrophobic interview rooms. Before he left, he would tell them what they needed to know.

Corrective Services weren't taking any chances: Glenn Abbott was no stranger to them, and if he was going outside the prison gates, it would be under the watchful eye of a four-man team from the Metropolitan Security Unit (MSU). One of them even sat in on the interview. Just to be sure.

Potter and Drown had planned it carefully. It was a key moment in the operation and they didn't intend to waste it. Glenn was an angry man when he arrived. He was there voluntarily, but was initially more interested in abusing his interviewers.

Potter took a back seat. Abbott already hated him and wasn't likely to change his mind. But Steve Drown was a new face to Abbott. He was 'Choko' to his colleagues, lover of rose gardens and cardigans, thirty years early. Smooth in an interview room, he remained friendly in the face of abuse. And good cop/bad cop wasn't an entirely Hollywood concept, given a bit of subtlety.

Over the next six hours, Drown would gently coax snippets of information from Glenn, but it wasn't easy. Touch the wrong subject and he'd clam up for hours. 'It was like treading a minefield,' Drown recalls. 'He went through a whole spectrum of emotions over the course of the interview. He was an erratic person to deal with.'

He was also worried. What would happen to him? And just what did these guys know? Drown was soothing, assuring him that something could be worked out. Slowly he relaxed, and eventually Drown had him laughing and joking. Next minute, he was in tears. He didn't want to be away from his family, he sobbed. Embarrassed, he asked the MSU guard to wait outside.

Then his mood turned again. Glenn Abbott enjoyed being the centre of attention, for a change. He began to open up. 'It almost seemed like he felt obliged to help us,' Drown says. 'He let slip that he had something hidden at "a place that no-one knows about".'

Later, after the detectives had finally milked some details from him, Steve Drown would go to Glenn's Honeywell storage

with the CS gas, caution had become the watchword. But the trunk and bag were safe. Inside were two sniper rifles, a Ruger and a Springfield, and a hefty supply of ammunition. There was also the receipt for the Pink Poodle Motel, which placed Glenn on the Gold Coast around the time of the break and enter on Gold Coast Shooters Supplies.

Eventually, Glenn would claim in court that Brenden had sent the guns without even telling him. The guns had arrived in Perth by courier a few days after the robbery, where they sat in the storage shed until Glenn, master criminal, opened his mouth in the interview room.

But it wasn't to be his biggest mistake that day. Drown carefully steered the conversation towards Brenden. Perhaps Glenn didn't realise the importance of what he was about to reveal. Or perhaps his family and his future were weighing heavily on his mind. If he offered them something small, something insignificant, maybe they could be tricked into giving him a better deal.

'Post Office Box 470, Mermaid Beach, on the Gold Coast. That's the only way I know how to contact him,' he told them. It was an important break. But it would be several weeks before the detectives and their Queensland counterparts had a chance to appreciate the moment. And later, Glenn would spend many hours reflecting on those crucial few moments in the interview room. He responded the only way he knew how, repeatedly threatening both officers' lives, consumed with shame by what he had done.

As soon as the interview ended, he swung into damage control, getting word to Kelly that the post office box was compromised. She got straight on the phone. 'Fat Boy stinks, PO box stinks. From Dirty Girl,' read the message on Brenden Abbott's pager at 6 pm. And then again, at 10 am the next day, the final message received: 'Correction. The old man stinks. Your post office box stinks and Fat Boy stinks. Regards, Dirty Girl.'

Not that it made any difference. As Abbott was soon to learn, it's one thing to stop using a post office box. It's entirely another to stop mail from being delivered to it. But he never really knew the truth of how he was caught, despite close questioning of detectives after his recapture. They weren't giving away free intelligence. Let him work it out for himself.

A version of the truth would eventually circulate: the police had found the address scrawled on a piece of paper at the Halls Head home. Glen Potter would smile to himself when the theory was repeated in the media. He knew what had really happened that day. 'Glenn rolled completely for his own purposes on the person he idolised most in the world,' he says. 'In prison, that's known as a real dog trick.'

The post office box address was passed on to Queensland, but for the moment, something more immediate had landed in the Western Australian detectives' laps. Abbott was back in town and running with some heavy duty bikies. So said a helpful informant who gave them an address and even drew on an Abbott mugshot to show his current appearance.

It was considered a reliable tip, and the surveillance operation shifted back into high gear. They eventually placed Abbott in a

Queensland after checking out his brother's now futile situation. It was the Western Australian detectives' last shot at recapturing him, at least during this investigation. With Brenden Abbott, there always seemed to be a next time.

Chapter 11

Recapture

'I fuckin' had you cunts shitting for a while, didn't I?'
— Brenden Abbott, face down and handcuffed
on a Gold Coast street, 11 am, 27 March 1995

Dirty Girl was right. By March 11, a hidden camera was keeping a watchful eye on Brenden Abbott's post office box at Mermaid Beach. Of course, he wasn't going within a mile of it, but detectives went through the tapes each day, waiting, hoping for something to appear inside. He checked the name and address the box had been registered to, expecting and finding both to be false.

Then, a few days later, manna from heaven — a pager bill arrived. Gerry Costello executed a search warrant and seized it. One warrant later, and they had the last three months' worth of messages received on the pager. Intelligence officers pored over the material, looking for a clue. Later, the messages would help form a picture of how Abbott and his associates communicated.

Glenn Abbott — using the name Michael — had been in touch regularly, enjoying the cloak and dagger of it all:

18 January 1995: 'Parcel sent. Hopefully rebore will go all right. Let me know if any problems. Michael.' [Guns.]

Second message: 'Verify received package with paper work and last message. Michael.' [More guns.]

29 January 1995: 'Friend has small motor. Value is $3000. Contact me if you want it. Only small block number. Michael.'

Second message: 'Serial number was FN765. Michael.'

Third message: 'Is second hand, in good condition Lowest price $2500. Michael.' [Sales pitch for a high-powered weapon.]

2 February 1995: 'Sent small motor on Monday. Should be there by now. Diff will be sent early next week. Let me know how you did down the quarter.'

Abbott had invested too much time and money for his cars simply to be showpieces. And consider his traffic record from Western Australia: speeding, driving under suspension, dangerous driving, speeding, demerit point suspension, contravene traffic signal, speeding, demerit point suspension, speeding, speeding, speeding, speeding. He liked to drive. Fast.

On 13 November 1992, he took part in Operation Drag, a police-sponsored race for Gold Coast petrolheads. Abbott entered one of his Holdens using a false Northern Territory driver's licence, but the motor wasn't quite right on the day. He lost.

3 February 1995: 'Made mistake on parcel. Only sent by standard road. Should be there early next week. Sorry for the inconvenience. Michael.'

Second message: 'Received pick. Works 100 per cent on everything I have tried. You can only wish to have one. Michael.' [A lock pick arriving in the mail.]

5 February 1995: 'Advertisement in Melbourne *Herald Sun* today. Regards, Freddie.' [Abbott had featured in an article in the Sunday *Herald Sun* that day.]

There were plenty of other messages too, and several women were in regular contact via the pager. It was one of these messages which would prove the vital link. Someone had been less than diligent in sticking to the codes. This led the detectives to an address in the heart of the Gold Coast: Unit 54, Florida Apartments, just a few metres from the beach at Surfers Paradise.

A surveillance team moved into an adjacent apartment building, setting up video equipment and waiting for a face to appear in the window. But when the detectives checked the footage and caught glimpses of a man's face, they realised they had a problem. Who knew what Brenden Abbott looked like on any given day? They needed to be sure.

On March 26, the National Crime Authority (NCA) lent the operation a specialist team. They would place surveillance devices in the apartment the next time its two occupants went out. It was a secure unit, with the only access via a key-entry lift. The occupant had also installed motion detectors and fitted a more secure lock to the front door, with the old lock transferred to a bedroom door. Getting in would take some doing. But for the moment, it was a moot point — the man in the apartment was in no hurry to go anywhere on this particular day. He'd been lying around on the floor most of the morning and didn't look like making a move. Just before 11 am, they watched as he began ironing a shirt and folding clothes. Then, a development: he began packing a bag.

'Target appears to be on the move,' the observation team alerted undercover officer Roman Quadvlieg, a detective senior constable attached to the NCA who was stationed outside the apartments.

A couple of minutes later, Quadvlieg watched a man in glasses, blue shorts and a white T-shirt walk out and turn into Fern Street. He was carrying bags in both hands and wearing a brown leather belt bag around the midriff.

Quadvlieg started his car and began following at a discreet distance. The man continued walking, turning right into Old Burleigh Road. Where was he off to? Could they afford to pass up this opportunity?

The officer turned the corner, passed the man, and parked about 60 metres further down the road. He turned and began walking back, preparing for the confrontation. Service revolver at the ready. He confronted the man near a bus stop. 'Police, get down on the ground now.'

Brenden Abbott hesitated, calculating his chances of reaching for the loaded .32 pistol in his belt bag. Quadvlieg moved quickly, grabbing Abbott's shoulder and pushing down hard. 'Down on the ground right now.' Abbott sunk to his knees, dropping both bags.

'Put both arms on the ground in front of you and keep them still.'

Another officer arrived, pistol drawn: 'What's your name?'

'Barry Fowler. My driver's licence is in my wallet. What's going on?' It was an optimistic line. They had already found the pistol.

'Where are you going?'

'My car. Why, what's going on?'

'That's not your name. Your name's Brenden Abbott. You're being detained under the provisions of the Weapons Act. Do you understand that?'

Abbott, accepting defeat, searched his prison vocabulary for the appropriate response. 'I fuckin' had you cunts shitting for a while, didn't I?'

Glen Prichard raced to the scene, finding it hard to believe the shadow he had been chasing had finally materialised. 'It felt good to finally see he was a real person, not just a figment of my imagination,' he recalls. 'Every time there was a creak in a bank roof, we'd think it was Abbott. We always seemed to be running around in circles trying to find him. It was good to see he actually existed.'

For all the Brisbane and Gold Coast detectives involved, this was their moment in the sun: they'd outwitted the nation's cleverest violent criminal. It was also a redemption, of sorts. Abbott's genuinely national operation had shown them all up, from Perth to Adelaide to Melbourne to the Gold Coast. By simply moving from state to state, and through a combination of commonsense, caution and luck, he had somehow avoided a focused, coordinated investigation. The 'postcards' and the 'up-yours' attitude aside, Abbott had embarrassed the police even more by robbing banks whenever the need or urge arose. And until Sid Thomas, Glen Prichard, Glen Potter and Gerry Costello put their heads together, no one had been prepared to face the scale of the problem.

Ultimately, Probe: Flanders would be considered a resounding success. All the detectives felt a sense of

and group certificates, scanners set to Gold Coast police frequencies, and a Colt .38 with loaded magazines, very similar to the one used in the Pacific Fair job. A 1984 Toyota LandCruiser was found near the apartment, and it was established that Abbott had bought it for $7 500 earlier that year, in a false name.

About $70 000 in cash was spread around the apartment, as well as a laminating machine, a piece of paper with police frequencies written on it, four Chubb security keys, and a rental document for a storage shed at Burleigh Heads. They weren't numbered, of course, and it took some shoe leather to establish that two of the keys fitted shed 351. It was empty.

Finally, the keys fitted shed 283, which held the answers to all their evidentiary problems. After the necessary warrants were obtained, they found electronics equipment, including televisions, stereos and surveillance devices, photographic gear for manufacturing false licences and backing sheets for Northern Territory driver's licences.

There were several bags which contained two Yaesu FC23 transceivers, two pairs of black gloves, two pairs of headsets with microphones, wigs, false moustaches, skin tone make-up, and glue used by make-up artists to attach props to the body. An FT26 transceiver minus the strap was also found, and would later be linked to the one left behind at the Pacific Fair bank.

The list was endless: locks — some with the barrels drilled, drill bits, a portable vice, key-cutting files, key blanks, a cordless drill kit, binoculars, and combinations for two safes, which have never been located.

There were also two small, battered address books with contact details for family and associates, and Abbott was furious when the police later refused to hand them back.

Costello and Detective Inspector Ray Platz, the Brisbane Armed Robbery Squad chief, interviewed Abbott at the Broadbeach police station. A photograph was taken and he didn't appear to be a happy camper in the bright Polaroid: they'd seized his $10 000 gold chain and expensive Tag Heuer watch. As usual, he 'wouldn't go to paper', but was still willing to have an informal chat.

'I've got plenty stashed away for a defence. I don't care if I spend everything I have stashed away. I'll fight you trial by trial. That's the system. Trial by judge and jury. I'd write a book about my life,' he joked, 'but the bloody government would take all the profits.' (Under the Proceeds of Crime Act.)

'Great idea,' said Costello. 'I'll help. We'll call it Abbott and Costello.'

It was all a bit of a giggle, it seemed, now that Abbott had regained his composure.

After the 'interview' ended he was transferred to the Southport watch house, chatting with his escorts on the way.

'If you're short of cash, don't worry,' he told them. 'I'm ripe for a loan.'

But that night, alone in his cell, the reality of it all would have sunk in: four walls, wash basin, prison bed.

A weary Glen Prichard arrived at the Southport court early the next morning, trying to put aside the events of the previous day, which had finally ended around 3 am. He had a trial starting that morning, but as he passed a cell in the watch house, Abbott called him over. There was something on his mind. 'How'd you catch me? Was it the public phone boxes? Did Glenn give me up?'

'I can't tell you that. What can you tell me about the $70 000 we found in your apartment?'

Abbott laughed. 'There's good money growing marijuana.'

Prichard, curious, asked what he'd done to relax while on the run. Abbott began talking cars, and warmed to the subject. After a few minutes on the intricacies of the V8 engine, he dropped another gem. 'I've had three speeding tickets too, in New South Wales. Used false licences and paid the fine straight away. No worries.'

Prichard had to leave, in a hurry to get to court. When he passed by later during an adjournment, Abbott was pacing the cell.

'What, are you trying to lose some weight?' Prichard asked him.

'Don't worry, I'll get on the weights while I'm in here. I'll get out and get square.'

'You look uptight, mate. What are you thinking about?'

Abbott smirked. 'Just planning my next escape.'

Prichard asked if he'd be willing to give a blood sample. He needed it to compare with the blood found on the wall after the Eleanora robbery. 'Not a chance. What's happened to all the property?'

'It'll be itemised and used in evidence.'

'What about the guns?'

'What guns?'

Prichard was incredulous. The shed search. How did he know about that already?

Abbott asked to make a phone call.

'Who do you want to ring?'

'My brother David.'

'Why?'

'He's the only one I can contact. Diane [his sister] has moved and got a silent number.'

He then began talking about his family, mentioning that he'd rung his mother in the early days but stopped, correctly suspecting the phone was tapped.

'So . . . did Glenn give me up? I heard he got arrested over guns and silencers and assault.'

'How do you know that?'

'I've got a contact who keeps me informed.'

'Where were you going yesterday?

'Cairns, from Coolangatta. Fly my own plane.'

Was he teasing? The theory that he had access to a plane and a false pilot's licence had been raised before.

'Nah, not really. I go first class on commercial flights.'

'How did you transport guns?'

'Just in bags. They were never checked. Brought a sub-machine gun back from Tasmania once.'

show in Victoria with plenty of cash in his pockets, he told Prichard, and bought several guns. Right under the nose of a bunch of federal coppers.

'So where've you been living?'

'Everywhere. Darwin, Alice Springs, Cairns. Bit of time in the bush, too.'

When things got too hot, he said, he liked throwing a swag in a LandCruiser and heading bush.

'So why'd you keep coming back to the Gold Coast?'

'I like it. It's still a quiet place when the tourists aren't around.'

But he admitted that, ultimately, returning had been a mistake which had helped lead to his downfall.

Prichard enquired about the false driver's licences.

'I put a lot of time and money into those. Did you see the artwork? I did all that by hand. Pretty good job, eh? It cost me a fortune to get the camera gear and get it all right.'

He returned to his favourite subject. 'So, did you trace the calls from the workshop in Cairns? How's my mate Dave?'

Prichard didn't know what the hell he was talking about. 'Dave', it would later be revealed, was David Male, a Cairns panelbeater Abbott was friendly with who had been working on one of the Holdens.

'He'll be shit scared when you go to see him. He didn't know who I was.'

Prichard tried fishing again. 'Where'd you pick up your electronics knowledge?'

'You'll have to do better than that,' Abbott replied. He might have been talkative, but he was still careful not to reveal details which could link him to specific crimes.

'He really opened up. I think he just wanted someone to chat to,' Prichard said later. 'It was the first chance he'd had to speak as Brenden James Abbott in a long time.'

But the timing wasn't good. Prichard had to get back to court again, and reluctantly left.

Abbott made a lasting impression on the young detective. 'I've never come across anyone who puts so much planning and work into what he does. He's obviously had a great deal of luck, but to some extent he's also made his own luck as well,' Prichard says. 'He's raised the level of sophistication of his trade and he learns from his mistakes.'

He quotes a hypothetical situation often used by detectives to sum up Abbott's manner: 'He's not a crook that stands out in the crowd, but if he walked into a pub in a country town and didn't know anyone at the bar, it'd be five minutes before someone was having a drink with him. He's a personable bloke and can talk at different levels depending on the company. He doesn't swear and curse and carry on like the average criminal.'

Prichard also noted that Abbott was cautious when it came to recreational drug use. He liked marijuana and its helpful paranoiac qualities, but that was as far as it usually went. He needed to stay in control and on guard. 'That's why he stayed off the drink. He didn't want to put himself in a bad situation,' Prichard says.

After the subsequent court saga, the detective and the criminal would meet again more than two years later. By then, Abbott had put in hard time in solitary, but the sly grin and the glint in the eyes were still there. He was simply waiting for the right moment.

half hours, in which time 'he went from absolutely no comment to a cheerful discussion of the case'.

'He wanted to know how he was caught, and in the course of the conversation let a few things slip about where he had been and what he had done,' Potter says.

Sid Thomas made his fruitless enquiry about Trevor Bailey's whereabouts, and Abbott laughed off all suggestions that he answer questions related to specific robberies. But he was happy to repeat and expand on the Boys' Own tales he had related to Prichard. He mentioned that one of his more valuable tools of trade while on the run had been a stolen South Australian police radio. If he suspected he was being followed — by police or otherwise — he assumed the role of Constable Abbott, calling up the details of cars from the police enquiry channel.

'He was well versed in police procedure,' says Potter. 'And he was already looking to gather more intelligence for his next escape. I viewed him as another experienced detective. He had a lot of the same attitudes and views on crime, but was on the wrong side of the fence.'

After the interview concluded, the detectives discussed their impressions and came to a common conclusion. 'It wasn't hard to work out what was going to happen,' says Potter. Abbott, they theorised, would try to prolong the judicial process to increase his number of court appearances — and hence increase his opportunities to escape. Once that became hopeless, he would plead guilty and then move into the general prison population. Then it would be a matter of waiting for his security rating to be downgraded and the appropriate opportunity to arise.

Reflecting on this prediction, Potter shakes his head. 'And that's exactly how it happened.'

Later that day, three decidedly more friendly visitors arrived at the prison. But the presence of Thelma Salmon, David Abbott and Kelly Fisher in Brisbane didn't go unnoticed.

A surveillance team followed David from the prison to the airport. After arriving in Cairns later that day, he was picked up by local detectives. The oldest of the Abbott brothers had been on his way to a storage unit near the airport, where one of Brenden's vehicles, a white Holden HQ utility, was recovered. He was also found in possession of $9000 cash, and charged with possession of tainted profits and concealing tainted property, under the Crimes (Confiscation of Profits) Act. David Abbott was convicted in Cairns Magistrates Court on 4 July 1995 and fined $3000. He was also ordered to forfeit the cash and car.

At the time, these developments prompted Glen Potter to comment to *The West Australian* that 'they're just like the bloody

not always a pleasant experience. Thelma Salmon may have been a suburban grandmother, but it wasn't uncommon for detectives to be accompanied by a Tactical Response Group team when knocking on her door. It was intimidating but necessary, in the detectives' view: you never knew who might be home.

But the constant police and media attention annoyed the family. Some may even have felt a secret sense of relief after Abbott's arrest. They had been concerned that the police wouldn't hesitate to shoot him, given the right opportunity. Now, he was at least safe from that fate. And there were no more raids, phone taps, surveillance, interviews or annoying calls from the media to worry about. Perhaps now, being related to Brenden Abbott would no longer be the dominant force in their lives.

Chapter 12

Trials and tribulations

'The offences were aimed at securing a sufficient amount of money for the prisoner to live out his days in another country . . . But unlike so many other offences of this sort, these were not motivated by drug addiction or psychological disorder but were the product of an individual who chose crime as a way of life.'

— Prosecutor Bernard Reilly,
Brisbane District Court, 2 May 1997

Abbott's reputation preceded him. The managers of the Arthur Gorrie Remand and Reception Centre in Brisbane sized him up and wisely decided that extra precautions would be needed. It was, after all, a remand centre, not a maximum security prison. But the 'special treatment' order they placed on him didn't come with VIP privileges. He was placed in a three-metre by three-metre cell and denied most normal inmate privileges and, consequently, escape opportunities.

Abbott wasn't taking that lying down. He immediately engaged the services of Chris Nyst, a high-profile Gold Coast lawyer. Nyst knew the value of the media, and throughout the

The prison managers were unimpressed. A Corrective Services report several years later summed up their reasoning: 'These arrangements were deemed appropriate in consideration of available intelligence which had been provided by several correctional and law enforcement agencies across the country. This information and intelligence indicated that Abbott posed an extremely high escape risk, arguably a higher risk than had ever been posed by a prisoner in the State of Queensland at that time.'

Nyst was undeterred. On April 9, he told the *Courier-Mail* that he had complained to the Criminal Justice Commission over the solitary confinement. This time he issued an ultimatum, saying he would take the matter to the Supreme Court unless his client was moved from solitary and given normal privileges by the next day. Arthur Gorrie general manager Greg Howden was having none of it.

The case did make it to the Supreme Court and, on July 19, Howden explained to Justice Paul de Jersey that a three-metre by three-metre cell, surrounded by two six-metre-high fences and electronic security devices, wasn't sufficient to keep Abbott secure.

Security in the court that day reinforced the caution — or perhaps paranoia — which Abbott had inspired. He was manacled with two pairs of handcuffs on his wrists and ankle shackles chained to a body belt. Armed police wearing earpieces were stationed around the building, and officers were on hand in the courtroom. Anyone entering the court had to pass two metal detectors. Abbott was separated from the public by a one-centimetre thick glass panel, and the seats directly behind him were removed. Never again would he — or brother Glenn — appear in court without a full-scale police and media circus.

It was almost embarrassing for the police, who came under fire from several quarters over the measures, but as one Western Australian detective would later point out, 'We were damned if we did and damned if we didn't.' Abbott could complain all he liked — they'd rather put on a spectacle and play it safe. During the Supreme Court hearing, Justice de Jersey asked Howden if his concerns were with the ability of the detention unit, or the centre, to hold high-security prisoners. 'Both,' he replied. 'It is not sufficient to hold a prisoner in my belief, of the calibre of this inmate.'

He said he had asked Corrective Services to transfer Abbott to another prison. They'd found drawings of lock mechanisms and weapons, drawn from memory, in his cell — not the type of inmate that inspired trust in prison management. Walter Sofronoff, a Queen's Counsel engaged by Abbott especially for the occasion, argued that the isolation was designed to pressure Abbott into a guilty plea. He also said the special treatment orders were only supposed to be imposed on prisoners for short periods.

The decision tested Abbott's patience, but he would have been consoled by one certainty — no one stays in solitary forever.

Chris Nyst opted for a committal hearing before going to trial on the robbery charges, a standard ploy to get a preview of the prosecution case. It was also a chance to grind some axes.

'Postcard Bandit sent cards by police and guards, court told,' read the headline in the *Courier-Mail* on 11 July 1995. It seemed the detectives and prison guards, for so long the straight men in Abbott's act, had finally turned the tables.

On the first day of the hearing, Nyst told the court that Abbott had received two postcards. The first, he said, was believed to be from Perth detectives, and read: 'Brendan [sic] baby, how are ya? Only one thing to say — Gotcha!'

The other card, believed to have been penned by prison guards, was a little deeper: 'Time waits for no man. Glad to see it's finally caught up with you. This is a dose of your own medicine.'

The senders would have been fully aware that there were never any postcards, but that only made the irony more delicious — and Abbott more annoyed. The police had encouraged this myth, Nyst said, so that his client was written up as 'the biggest criminal, the biggest bushranger, since Ned Kelly'. Continued protestations on the issue by Abbott — 'I didn't send them any bloody postcards' — would prove fruitless. No deed poll could change a name christened in the media, whatever the facts.

Nyst also had a few other bones to pick on the first day of the hearing, held at Southport Magistrates Court on the Gold Coast. Abbott — who would be taken to court in a helicopter on numerous occasions — again appeared with knees shackled and hands secured to a body belt by two sets of handcuffs. Police were stationed on nearby rooftops, and everyone entering the courtroom passed a metal detector. A contingent of plain clothes officers in the court completed the now-standard full-scale security operation.

'He's trussed up like Hannibal Lecter ... he looks like Terminator III,' Nyst spluttered, motioning at his client. Shackling Abbott was 'an affront to the system of justice which presumes innocence', he said. But the magistrate ruled that the shackles were 'appropriate to the circumstances'.

The next day — after he'd hand-fed them the story — Nyst directed his fury at the media, claiming they had placed 'an aura of guilt' around his client and should be banned from the court. The 'lurid' publication of court security arrangements portrayed him as 'a dangerous and sinister person' and the 'level of press manipulation was a scandal'.

Nyst said that the publication of photos of Abbott and references to him being the Postcard Bandit were prejudicial. Annoyed, prosecutor Bernard Reilly accused Nyst of grandstanding, pointing out that he was the one who had been appearing on television and sprouting 'Hannibal Lecter' lines.

Even so, Nyst had a point. Identification of suspects is a key issue in armed robbery cases, and publishing pictures could easily compromise witness recollections.

Over the course of the investigation, it would be one of many problems the media caused for both sides.

The previous month, this book's author had earned Nyst's wrath after an article appeared in *Australian Penthouse*. The magazine had purchased the story from *The West Australian* several months before Abbott's recapture. But the lengthy delay between deadline and arrival of the magazine from an overseas printer meant that Abbott had already been caught by the time the magazine hit the stands. A rewrite by *Penthouse* had left it riddled with errors (the standard gripe of all reporters) and it was also highly prejudicial now that Abbott was before the courts.

But Nyst's objections to the media coverage were brushed aside by Magistrate Marshall Davies, who said it had no bearing on the committal proceedings.

The detectives, too, had their share of run-ins with the media. Gerry Costello always maintained that officers in other states released too much information over the course of the investigation, greatly hindering his state's inquiries. The inadvertent release of the picture of Abbott found in the Tweed Heads storage shed, for example, caused a major headache. It was the key photograph used in witness identifications over the Pacific Fair robbery, and Abbott's defence team would later create havoc with the issue in court. Not surprisingly, Costello developed an aversion to journalists and played his cards close to his chest.

The media could be useful, but sometimes their loose-cannon qualities just weren't worth the consequences.

The four-week hearing wouldn't be completed for months, fragmented by frequent adjournments and Magistrate Marshall Davies suffering a heart attack.

At one point, a game inmate whose identity was suppressed agreed to give evidence of a conversation he claimed to have had with Abbott in prison. He testified that they had become friendly, and he had taken notes of a conversation dealing with Abbott's 'nefarious activities from one side of Australia to the other'. He said Abbott told him that the Pacific Fair job had been Australia's biggest bank robbery and netted $750 000.

When Reilly asked whether Abbott had said who was responsible, the witness replied: 'He said he was.' Abbott also allegedly told him that he had robbed four other Queensland banks, as well as banks in South Australia and Western Australia. He was a friendly bloke, the witness said, who took an interest in other prisoners' criminal histories. Admirers would often pass him magazines, chocolate and chips.

Abbott had a friend on the outside, too: Chris Nyst's service didn't come cheaply, and there was speculation about just where the money was coming from.

Brisbane's *Sunday Mail* made some enquiries in July 1995, but a legal Aid spokeswoman said that privacy considerations

were imposed on Abbott over the proceeds still missing from the three Queensland robberies of which he was convicted. The order gave detectives on Abbott's money trail more power to investigate his financial dealings. It also opened the book on Nyst's records: David Abbott, ever loyal, had been paying the bills.

Brenden Abbott finally faced trial — initially over the last robbery, at Eleanora — in May 1996. He'd spent a lot of time in the judicial system by now, and fancied his talents as a jailhouse lawyer and amateur psychologist. This time, as on several other occasions, he would insist on conducting his own jury selection. He took it seriously, exhausting the allowed number of challenges to potential jurors.

During the trial, the complaints about the shackles, chains

and security operation went unheeded, but evidence of it had to be hidden from the jury. Three of the five officers in court were in plain clothes, and the efforts to silence Abbott's rattling chains — lest the jury hear them — bordered on the comical.

Abbott's defence team could only chip around the edges of the prosecution's evidence, which was circumstantial but comprehensive. Bernard Reilly built a detailed case, even noting Glenn Abbott's movements around the nation. This prompted Judge Hoath to enquire: 'It is not suggested his brother is the other person involved in the robbery?'

Reilly: 'That may well be the case. The Crown can't say that that is the case one way or the other. However, given the contact between them prior and afterwards there does exist an inference that he could have been involved.'

The case would turn on a single piece of evidence which removed any doubt about one of the bandits' identities: blood found on a wall at the bank. A DNA comparison with a sample taken from Abbott matched the evidence, and Abbott's only hope lay with destroying its credibility. His lawyers took a sledgehammer to the chain of evidence, looking for weak links.

Initially, they raised doubts about the discovery of the blood: it wasn't easily visible and had been missed by the forensics team. Glen Prichard had noticed it days later. This prompted the first of several conspiracy theories, all with the same conclusion: someone had tampered with the evidence. Dennis Lynch, for Abbott, suggested that the thoroughness of the robbery investigations had been excessive. Could someone have overstepped the mark?

'Would you accept . . . that no stone has been left unturned in putting the brief together to ensure that Mr Abbott is convicted of this offence?' he asked Prichard, who was in the witness box.

there's always something else that could be done, to be honest.'

And just why did an armed robber rate the services of several surveillance teams, including one from the NCA? According to the detectives, the NCA team was required because of a shortage of available officers — even the Special Emergency Response Team wasn't available on the day — and the expertise required in setting up the surveillance.

Gerry Costello was confronted with a line of questioning similar to Prichard's, this time over the blood sample he took from Abbott. Things got a bit personal, with Lynch attacking the detective's character; his boss, Ray Platz, copped the same treatment. Even staff from the hospital where the sample was delivered were called to the witness box.

It was all to no avail. The chain of evidence stood firm and he was found guilty. In sentencing Abbott to nine years' jail, on 7 June 1996, Judge Hoath reluctantly noted: 'I must take into account the aggregate of the terms of imprisonment that you will have to serve. The effect is that in order to do justice to you I am obliged to impose a sentence which may, in isolation, appear to fail to reflect adequately the seriousness of the offence for which you have just been convicted.'

It was a line Abbott heard in court regularly over the years: his long history, and the ever-increasing number of years he owed the prison system, meant that a long jail term for another similar crime would be considered 'crushing'. In the long term, this meant Abbott actually seemed to get lighter sentences despite his increasingly serious record. But it probably made no difference in his mind. Since the Fremantle escape, he'd considered even a single day behind bars too long.

Lynch would later tell a court that when he visited Abbott after sentencing, his client indicated that he wanted to come to an arrangement with the DPP over the remaining charges. There were discussions with Bernard Reilly, who was receptive to the idea, but when Lynch returned to see Abbott, he refused to continue negotiations because of the security measures.

A few months after sentencing, Howden's wish was granted and Abbott was transferred to the Sir David Longland Correctional Centre, at south suburban Wacol in Brisbane. For the first month, he was held in virtual isolation, every move watched by a surveillance camera in the cell. There was then a transfer to more open cells in B Block, but it only lasted two and a half months. He was returned to the detention unit, then to a punishment cell which was later described by his lawyers as 'filthy and Spartan'.

Finally, Abbott's complaints to Corrective Services were heeded, and he was eased into the prison mainstream. He had complained long and hard to the authorities about his treatment, but in prison he earned a reputation as a stoic.

'At his lowest ebb in solitary confinement, sick and flabby from lack of exercise and desperate for human contact, he was allowed a rare phone call from Diane,' *Good Weekend* reported in April 1998.

'I asked how they were treating him,' she recalls.

'He said, "Like a king, sis! They treat me like a king".'

But Greg Howden, interviewed on Channel Seven's *Witness* program in 1998, painted a different picture.

'My experience of him was that he was not a hard man.'

'What, weak? Soft?' the interviewer asked.

'Yeah, basically weak . . . basically not in charge of himself sufficiently to be able to do jail.'

And yet Abbott knew the limestone confines of Fremantle Prison well, and would go on to endure many more months of solitary in Queensland.

He could do time. He just didn't like it.

The court battles — an epic circus by any standard — finally concluded in May 1997.

In the Brisbane Supreme Court on April 29, Judge Pratt ruled that the case was compelling enough for five of the remaining six charges to be tried on the similar fact evidence. It wasn't what Abbott wanted to hear. He asked for a short adjournment and, 53 minutes later, accepted the prosecution offer on the table. He would plead guilty to the Springwood and Pacific Fair robberies, and the remaining charges would be dropped.

On May 2, Bernard Reilly laid it all on the table in a formal but compelling and detailed sentencing submission.

> *In essence, it is submitted that . . . the robberies . . . were conducted by the prisoner to fund his existence whilst he continued to remain a fugitive from justice, that he had no legitimate forms of income, that his being unlawfully at large, particularly with police obviously searching for him, required him to expend substantial sums of cash.*
>
> *The Crown's submission is that the offences were aimed at securing a sufficient amount of money for the prisoner to live out his days in another country where*

*he need never have to answer for his misconduct. But
unlike so many other offences of this sort, these were
not motivated by drug addiction or psychological
disorder but were the product of an individual who
chose crime as a way of life.*

*Although it may be suggested by my learned friend
that the more professional a bandit's manner is, the less
trauma may be caused to his victims. This is not
something which necessarily follows and, indeed, the
cold and calculated manner in which the prisoner
committed these offences have [sic] left many of the
bank staff with psychological problems.*

*Staff who had not just to endure the commission of the
offences but then live with the memory of staring down
the barrel of the gun with the possibility of retribution at
the hands of a man desperate to avoid justice.*

He went on to detail the suffering — both immediate and long
term — of the staff involved in the robberies. They had the added
indignity, he said, of initially coming under suspicion after the
robbery because of the level of planning and knowledge
required. Some even blamed themselves for not noticing
anything wrong with the security procedures.

In reply to Reilly, Dennis Lynch, for Abbott, tendered three
psychological reports to the court. A correctional counsellor had
said Abbott's mental state had been adversely affected by the
isolation in prison.

'She says that since his transfer to C Block at the Sir David
Longland Centre only a couple of weeks ago that there has been a
remarkable change in him. She describes him as a different person

who no longer suffers from signs of depression,' Lynch said.

Of course he'd been depressed. But it was only the opportunity to escape, not Prozac, which would cure his melancholia.

Judge Pratt faced a difficult task sentencing Abbott that day. As well as the sentence that had already been imposed for the Eleanora robbery, he had over 12 years to serve of his Western Australian sentence. And there was still the pending matters of the escape, the swag of charges which could be laid over the 'summer holiday' and the warrant for the Glenelg robbery in South Australia.

Whatever the sentence, it seemed Abbott was destined for a life behind bars. The Crown wanted an extra three years added to the nine years for Eleanora. Judge Pratt settled on nine years for the Springwood robbery and ten years for Pacific Fair. They were to be served concurrently with the Eleanora sentence — in essence, an extra year's jail.

But musing over the figures, the judge noted that 'unless my arithmetic is completely shredded I think it's 60 we're looking at by the time he walks about a free man again'.

A lengthier sentence seemed unnecessary — the term was already sufficiently crushing. Judge Pratt went on to describe Abbott as a 'studied, disciplined, intelligent bank robber' — words of praise for a criminal rarely heard from the bench.

'Few people would accept that the mind which was capable of perpetrating these robberies is not also capable of, as it were, salting away for later use, large sums of money. All the evidence suggests that he is quite capable of doing that and probably has.'

But it would take more than money to buy freedom. It was time to indenture some new apprentices.

Deja vu

> *'I love you doll, love the kids; I don't think I'm going to
> make it this time.'*
> — Glenn Abbott, clutching a mobile phone and critically
>   injured from gunshot wounds, Perth, 6 September 1996

Over in Perth, Glenn Abbott had been busy fighting his own
court battles. His record and the seriousness of the incident
involving the Division 79 officers in 1995 had left him facing a
lengthy stretch in Casuarina Prison.

There were a raft of charges over the CS gas attack, the
weapons in his car and the arsenal at his Halls Head home. But
there was much debate between the police and lawyers at the
office of the Director of Public Prosecutions over the incident
involving Graham Randall's gun. Eventually, the lawyers settled
on a charge of assault to prevent arrest with intent to cause
grievous bodily harm.

'We thought that was piss weak. It was attempted murder, as
far as I was concerned,' Graham Randall says bluntly.

Doug Nelson agrees. 'They [the DPP] told us there was
no corroborating evidence. But there was the physical evidence

Glenn Abbott resulted in many sleepless nights after the attack, punctuated by nightmares in which he relived a twisted version of the events. With a service revolver pressed against his chest, and believing death was seconds away, Randall's first thought had been for his young daughter. His subconscious twisted this memory, and he would be woken by the horrifying image of himself shooting her with a service revolver. 'That sort of thing really gets you worried. I went to a police psychologist twice after it happened,' he recalls.

But he had little time to come to terms with the emotional repercussions of the attack. Randall's application to join the Canine Section had been accepted, and four weeks after the roadside battle, he was shipped off to New Zealand to train with his new partner. It was a difficult period, away from family and professional support when he needed it the most. Halfway through the course, he returned home.

Unaware that he was suffering from post-traumatic stress disorder, he continued to work, but things didn't get any easier with the shift to the Canine Section's office at the Western Australian Police Academy. Within a week of returning to duty, he was attacked with pepper spray and his dog was stabbed. 'I didn't really know what was happening to me. I was short-tempered, depressed and angry,' Randall says. 'Every time I pulled a car over, there was a thought that it might happen again.'

It took time, but he would eventually conquer his demons and build a successful career with the Canine Section. Letting Glenn Abbott think he had got the better of him was never an option. 'I wouldn't give the bastard the satisfaction,' he says.

But the sentence meted out to his attacker did nothing to help quell his anger. After receiving a total of two years, three months, Abbott was released in less than a year. And while Randall felt let down on a personal level, he and Doug Nelson felt there was another compelling reason to send Glenn Abbott away for as long as possible: he was simply too dangerous to be on the streets.

'Glenn tries to live up to his brother's reputation, but he just doesn't have the same coolness about him,' Nelson says. 'He's very intelligent, but he's not smart. They're two different things. He tends to let his emotions get the better of him when he's put under pressure . . . he's very good with things like guns and computers and fake IDs, but he's got a quick temper and is emotionally unstable. In a way, we were lucky that he chose the course of action that he did. If he'd come out with the gun instead of the pepper spray, we both would have been dead.'

Glenn Abbott had a lot on his mind after his release on parole. With Brenden behind bars, he feared he was now a prime target for 'toe cutters'. 'Toe cutting' — the cleanest, purest form of crime, according to Mark 'Chopper' Read — generally involves the kidnap of armed robbers by other criminals. Less than gentle methods of persuasion are then applied until the robber reveals where the proceeds are hidden, or dies. Whichever comes first.

Watch your back, Brenden warned Glenn from his Brisbane prison cell. Then the hand-up phone calls started. One anonymous caller asked if he was Brenden Abbott's brother. Glenn was worried — not only for himself, but for his young family. When an automatic pistol was sent from Queensland, he began carrying it. Just in case.

The pistol was close at hand as he sped down Tonkin Highway, in Perth's central suburban Bayswater, early in the afternoon of 6 September 1996. It was a 60 kilometres an hour zone, but he had the Commodore station wagon's V8 stretched out to about 160 kilometres an hour. Lee Watson, a 32-year-old senior constable based at Cannington, wasn't actively searching for traffic offenders that day — he was on his way to be fitted for a new leather jacket. But 160 in a 60 zone just couldn't be ignored. He gave chase, and Abbott pulled to a stop on Guildford Road. Two men in a roadsweeper were just ten-metres away. They would be crucial witnesses to the short, shocking exchange that was about to occur.

The criminal and the police officer exited their cars and began talking on the roadside. Lee Watson remembers asking routine questions — licence details, who owns the car — until he noticed two long objects in the motorist's jeans. 'Empty your pockets,' he told Abbott.

It was a magazine. Watson saw a cartridge protruding from the top, heard a loud bang and felt a pain in his left hip. There, his memory tapers off.

Glenn Abbott remembers it differently. 'He shot me first — he pulled his gun out, I pulled my gun out — he shot me first,' he insisted in the back of an ambulance a few minutes later.

If that were the case, Glenn was awesomely prepared for such a situation — he had 14 rounds of ammunition in his pocket, a magazine with 15 cartridges was later found on the ground, and there were 16 rounds in the gun.

Ian Robinson — in the roadsweeper a few metres away — had watched Abbott speak to Watson, return to his car and then hand the officer a black object. 'All of a sudden he lunged at the cop and as the cop was falling back, his right hand went down to his hip. As he went down there was a crack, then there were four or five bangs,' he would later tell a court.

But — crucially — did he hear the sound as the officer was reaching for his holster? Yes, as he reached for the holster, Robinson would answer the prosecutor.

Glenn's pistol, a Glock, was dirty and corroded and — fortunately for Lee Watson — jammed after the first round was fired. In later test firings by police, it misfired one in five times. Ballistic experts theorised that it may have jammed because of the oversized magazine or the shooter's hand obstructing the sliding mechanism. Either way, it probably saved Lee Watson's life. His single wound wasn't life-threatening, but it was a close thing. The accident and emergency doctor who treated Watson says the entry wound was a centimetre from the main artery in his left leg. If it had been pierced, he could have bled to death in six minutes.

Laurie Biggs, another witness parked across the road, heard the incident before he saw it. 'There was the first one, then a short break,' he would tell a court. 'Then a pop, pop — then a short break — then a pop, pop, pop, pop.'

disappeared so I went back to the cop.'

But Glenn was going nowhere. Three of Watson's shots had found their mark, with one passing through his left leg. Oddly, the other two travelled vertically through his body. One entered near the right nipple and passed through the liver and bowel before lodging on the left side of his pelvis. The second travelled from Abbott's right abdomen down into the right side of his pelvis. Gunpowder marks on his arm indicated that the shots had been fired at close range.

He returned to his car and tried to escape, but was blocked in by the roadsweeper. Abbott then walked over to Lee Watson, whose welfare now seemed to be his paramount concern, despite his own critical wounds. Ian Robinson and his partner Mark Baker had jumped from the roadsweeper and were tending to the officer's hip wound. 'Is he OK?' Glenn asked them before collapsing to the ground.

'He fell down and that's when we noticed his shirt was covered in blood,' Ian Robinson says. 'When I opened it up, he was full of holes.'

Glenn fumbled for his mobile phone, convinced he was about to die. He wanted to say goodbye to Kelly. 'I love you doll, love the kids; I don't think I'm going to make it this time,' he told her.

Lee Watson had managed to radio for help. By now, police were descending on the scene, responding to the most serious of calls — 'Member down'.

Glenn, now on the verge of tears, asked Constable Dominic Licastro if Watson was going to make it. 'I didn't mean it — tell him.' He began to sob. 'Is he going to be all right? I'm sorry. I'm a criminal, mate, not a killer. I didn't mean to. I was pressured into it. If I go, I'm sorry.'

During the ambulance ride to Royal Perth Hospital, Abbott regained his composure and began insisting that Watson had fired the first shot.

Abbott's guard, Constable Paul Carter, asked, 'Why did he shoot you?'

'He asked me to empty my pockets. I pulled a clip out, he pulled his gun out and we started to shoot.'

'What's your name?'

'I'm Brenden Abbott's brother — you should know him.'

'Why were you carrying a gun?'

'I don't know. I've got a lot of problems at the moment.'

Graham Randall, just a few minutes away from the shooting scene at the police academy in Maylands, was among the officers who responded to the shooting. Initially, the call had been for an unknown offender fleeing into bushland. He made straight for the scene with his dog, but Abbott was already on the way to the hospital by the time he arrived.

'Do you know who that was?' another officer at the scene asked him.

'No. Who?'

'It's your mate from last year.'

'We warned them,' Randall thought to himself. 'But they wouldn't bloody listen.'

Glenn Abbott was lucky to survive the ride to hospital. He was resuscitated several times before reaching an operating table, where surgeons worked feverishly for several hours. It would take months, but Abbott would eventually recover, the scars criss-crossing his body a testament to his brush with death.

At the other end of the continent, his older brother must have been shaking his head. Would Glenn never learn? This time around, he would have plenty of time to reflect on his mistake; there would be no quick exit from Casuarina. But even inside, away from the toe cutters and police, Glenn Abbott wouldn't be safe from his greatest enemy — himself.

Chapter 14

Whatever it takes

'You can never give up trying, can you?'
— Brenden Abbott's response to a detective's observation
that he seemed to be gathering intelligence
for an escape, Brisbane, 22 May 1997

It was no secret that Brenden Abbott wanted out. Even before he was shifted from the Arthur Gorrie Remand and Reception Centre, word had spread that he was prepared to pay big money for the right sort of assistance — preferably ex-military. Depending on who you spoke to, the figure Abbott was offering ranged from $50 000 to $100 000. But if there were any takers, none stepped forward before his transfer to Sir David Longland Correctional Centre (SDL) at Wacol.

Abbott arrived in September 1996, about two months after being sentenced on the Gold Coast robbery charges. Arthur Gorrie management were glad to see the back of him. They had been under no illusions about who they were dealing with and had gone to extraordinary lengths to limit his escape opportunities. A detailed intelligence profile was provided to SDL management, who initially treated him with the same caution.

(QCSC) spokesman actually boasted that the department was 'one step ahead' of prisoners like Abbott. 'The QCSC regularly identifies inmates it considers to be of high risk of escape. They are placed on special observation,' he said. 'There is a unit at Woodford Correctional Centre for inmates who require "special management". An example of this type of inmate is Brenden Abbott.'

Abbott took it as a challenge and began setting up an escape plan in advance, allegedly involving guns-for-hire from a notorious motorcycle club. But Woodford management wanted to iron out some wrinkles in the new set-up before being sure of staying 'one step ahead'; the transfer was never approved.

Abbott didn't mind. Slowly, he had been gathering the necessary ingredients to move a step ahead of the Sir David Longland staff. After waiting patiently through the long stints in solitary, his depression disappeared as his privileges were increased.

The idea of another chance at freedom restored the sly twist to his grin, and Glen Prichard took note of his demeanour when he visited the prison on 22 May 1997. He was there to discuss the forfeiture order granted by the court, but, not surprisingly, Abbott wasn't interested in revealing where any of his assets were hidden. And he was indignant at the suggestion that he forfeit his Tag Heuer watch and $10 000 gold chain — both seized when he was arrested — insisting they had been gifts. Abbott also demanded the return of the two small, battered address books which had served him so well while on the run. There was no reason they couldn't come in handy again in the future.

When the conversation eventually turned to the case, Abbott became expansive, volunteering that he'd 'be lucky to have $500 000 left' from bank robberies. Leaving blood behind at the scene of the Eleanora robbery had pissed him off, he commented. The issue of Trevor Bailey's disappearance prompted only a laugh and a comment that nothing could be proved. And if South Australia wanted to extradite him over the Glenelg robbery, forget it. He'd fight them all the way.

He also mentioned how he'd felt safe staying at the Pink Poodle Motel after the Pacific Fair robbery, but had later made an interesting discovery among police records during trial preparations. 'I saw the running sheets. You got close while I was at the Pink Poodle,' he noted, intrigued by the details of the investigation.

Throughout the 45-minute exchange, Abbott continued to probe unashamedly for details on police methods and intelligence. 'Sounds like you're just trying to improve for next time,' Prichard told him.

Abbott smiled. 'You can never give up trying, can you?'

A lot of things would have to go Abbott's way if an escape was to succeed, but several factors were already conducive to the plan. His cell was virtually identical to those at Arthur Gorrie, where he'd spent 18 months. If there were weaknesses in the layout which could be exploited, he would know them well. And while he'd lacked easy access to visitors at Arthur Gorrie,

smuggle the necessary items into the prison.

His movements, like other inmates', were governed by a prison management plan, which in his case had the specific objectives of 'reducing the risk of escape and maximising personal program objectives within a secure environment'. It reflected the relaxation in Abbott's treatment, and on 8 September 1997, a new plan, effective for three months, brought new gains.

As well as contact visits, he was now allowed out of his cell for 11 hours a day, access to the health centre, normal meals, exercise time in the Unit 4B yard, and even access to the oval and gym at the discretion of the B Block supervisor.

In a decision later described as 'highly questionable' by prison inspectors, he was also made education clerk and allowed access to the education facilities. Abbott made full use of the phone in the education centre, making several unmonitored and unauthorised calls to help set the escape plan in motion. It was rumoured he was offering up to $50 000 for a mobile phone as well.

Such a complex plan required many irons in the fire, and leaks were hard to stop. The first whispers came just over two weeks after the new management plan was put in place. Intelligence indicated that several prisoners were to be busted out of Townsville Correctional Centre by a team of hired guns. They would then travel to Brisbane and break out Abbott and Jason John Nixon, a dangerous young criminal who had been convicted of killing another inmate.

The Townsville plot was thwarted and several inmates were transferred. Abbott's management was reviewed, but other than a directive that it be 'strictly adhered to', the escape plan prompted no changes.

But it was always a matter of when, not if, Abbott would try again. His willingness to learn from mistakes was a hallmark, and history had shown that he treated initial failure as a challenge rather than automatic defeat. Unperturbed, he began devising a new strategy.

Brendan Luke Berichon couldn't wait to tell his mum when she visited. 'Do you know the Postcard Bandit? I'm in with him. We're in the same cell block,' he told her during a visit.

It was the reaction of a starstruck kid. And, at age 20, that's all he really was. But unlike many of the young men enlisted by Abbott over the years, Berichon had made a genuine effort to steer his life away from crime.

His parents separated shortly after his birth in Newcastle on 30 December 1977, and he moved to Townsville with his mother, Julie, and older sister, Linda. His mother remarried several years later and the family expanded to three boys and a girl — a normal suburban family with no criminal connections. While they remained in Townsville, there were no problems with the good-natured boy who did well at school and enjoyed sport. But when the family moved to southern suburban Brisbane in 1988, things quickly started to go wrong. Drugs and 'the wrong crowd' — the two greatest fears of every parent — soon changed the good-natured, likeable boy into a truant and thief.

It was all downhill after he arrived at Sunnybank High School, Julie Berichon would later tell the *Courier-Mail*. 'He started wagging school, he tried marijuana. I heard there were

went out the window … He got into the drugs again,' Mrs Berichon said. 'He had the opportunity and he lost it.'

The result was inevitable. His growing drug habit led to a two-year sentence for armed robbery and other offences in 1996. Aged 17, he was sent to Sir David Longland and moved into the mainstream population after his next birthday. After being released, a parole violation landed him in B Block alongside the fabled Postcard Bandit. Spellbound by tales of life on the run, he must have felt honoured when Abbott decided to bring him in on the new escape plan.

Despite his usual attitude towards drug users, Abbott could see compelling reasons to make an exception in Berichon's case. He was serving a relatively short sentence, and could be well-briefed before release on how to arrange outside assistance. Berichon's fascination had also inspired an unswerving loyalty to Abbott — a trait which he couldn't help but admire — and he was also a fast learner.

After being released on 17 September 1997, Berichon began making discreet preparations, but he was careful not to arouse suspicions. After moving in with some friends, he gave every indication of wanting to part ways with crime. 'All I want is a family, a job and a home,' he told relatives.

His mother had lunch with him shortly after his release and nothing seemed amiss. She remembers his enthusiasm for a family get-together planned for Christmas in Townsville. 'The last time I saw him he gave me a hug and he said: "You'll see about those tickets to Townsville, Mum?" I said, "Yes." That was the last thing I said to him.'

As the events of the next few months unfolded, it became difficult for her to believe she would ever see him alive again.

Abbott had also begun preparations, putting together the internal phase of the operation. Using the same methodical approach applied to bank robbery, he puzzled over each challenge presented by the prison security until a solution could be found.

After deciding that a night-time operation had the best chance of success, he confronted his first and most obvious hurdle — escaping the cell undetected after lockdown. Abbott researched the subject well, discovering that angel wire, a diamond-

shops and was relatively cheap. Now it was just a matter of getting it into the prison.

He became friendly with armed robber Garry Merrick, the unit's prison cook, who received regular visits from his girlfriend, Natalee Hunter. The 24-year-old mother-of-one was more than willing to help out when she was approached, and even had the wire cut to size after buying it from a hardware store in suburban Ipswich. It was then secreted in her vagina so she could pass the security check on her way into the prison. Once in the visitor's room, Hunter was able to remove the wire and pass it through a small hole which had been made in a screen prior to her visit.

Abbott was appreciative of her efforts and signed over to her his television and stereo, which had earlier been found to have an unexplained hole in its back cover. Police later confiscated both items and charged Hunter, who would serve several months for her role in aiding the escape. In spite of this, she remained unrepentant. Abbott was a great bloke, she said, a friendly guy who was funny and charming. Why not help him out?

As November neared, the escape operation began to gain momentum. Abbott was making good use of the phone in the education centre, coordinating and arranging the operation on both sides of the perimeter fence.

There were also indications that he had gained access to a mobile phone, and late in October, a part-time prison intelligence officer reported straight to management after monitoring one of

Abbott's calls. This guy's getting ready to make a move, he warned them, and a search of Abbott's cell was immediately ordered. But nothing was found, and a routine check of B Block's cell bars on October 31 revealed no irregularities.

Abbott was managing to stay one step ahead, and with no moves to increase security, he pressed on with the last-minute details. Other prisoners had now been recruited, but his motives for including them were shrewd rather than generous. With serious injury a real possibility during the escape, it seemed sensible to minimise the risk by opting for safety in numbers. And their involvement could help divert the spotlight from Abbott, who knew his notoriety would now prevent him from fading quietly into the background again. His face and its various appearances were well-known, and another round of intense media coverage could only make anonymity more difficult.

With these considerations in mind, he assembled a particularly brutal group of criminals — three killers and a rapist — to make up the numbers. With a litany of senseless violence on their criminal records, they were sure to attract plenty of attention. Abbott, the publicly popular armed robber, would appear almost angelic by comparison.

If things went to plan, they would create havoc in Brisbane for a few days while he slipped away to resume his covert existence. Without the skills and temperament to stay on the run, it seemed unlikely they could remain at large for long.

Abbott's chances were a lot better considering his track record and intelligence, which had been gauged at 140 in an IQ test conducted at Arthur Gorrie. Given his image as a criminal mastermind, it was an interesting statistic which dropped short of

After later being questioned, he was released, but a troubled conscience led to a murder charge a few months later. It came after the troubled killer confided to another prisoner at a New South Wales jail that he was plagued by dreams of Sandra MacKay. In them, she would walk towards him, arms outstretched and dressed in white. Her family, also haunted, called for the return of the death penalty, but eventually, a mandatory life sentence was imposed in May 1988.

Alincic's violent behaviour continued in prison, where he became a regular troublemaker. On his record were convictions for four counts of wilfully damaging prison property, one of possessing a prohibited article and two more of unlawful assault.

Then there were the escape attempts. In 1990, Alincic had used a hacksaw to escape from his cell in a short-lived bid for freedom at Townsville Jail. They found him hiding on a construction site, still in the prison grounds. In 1996, Alincic was one of five prisoners who hijacked a tractor in an ill-fated attempt to escape from Borallon Jail, south of Ipswich in Brisbane. Chagrined, he claimed a prison van had run him over during the incident and tried to sue for damages. Now aged 30, he had arrived at Sir David Longland in November 1996 and was a high-security prisoner in B Block along with Abbott.

The second member of the escape team was Jason Nixon, a 27-year-old with an extensive criminal history that included serious assault and armed robbery. He had previously escaped in 1991 while on remand in Brisbane Jail over charges of harbouring an escapee and drug possession. A 20-year-old at the time, Nixon and three others used a garbage compactor truck to smash a set of gates and two solid steel doors to escape. He was recaptured and sent to Sir David Longland, where, in 1993, he confirmed his path in life during an incident in the prison gym. Armed with a bar bell, he attacked Bart Vosmaer, a connected criminal with a reputation behind bars as an enforcer. The attack was fatally brutal, inflicting massive fractures to his skull, knee caps, and an arm and a leg.

Andrew John Jeffrey, 20, was the third and final killer selected for the escape. Unlike the others, there was no lengthy criminal record, but his single major crime had been described by a judge as 'a vicious, cowardly attack on a defenceless man'. In December 1994, he was one of three young men who attacked a building company foreman who had unwisely promised to procure them some marijuana. They bashed and kicked him to death when he failed to deliver, resulting in a murder conviction and residence in B Block for Jeffrey.

armed robbery and deprivation of liberty. He later claimed he was only brought in on the escape at the last minute.

On the evening of 4 November 1997, the four were together in B Block, where overcrowding had forced the doubling up of prisoners. Alincic and Nixon were in cell 14, and Jeffrey and Stirling in cell 10, all waiting for the word. Abbott, alone in cell 12, was filling in a prison request form. His Postcard Bandit image — and the occasion — seemed to demand a special touch. Prison officers would later find it in the cell — reportedly pinned to the bunk with a 'smiley face'. In it was a request for immediate transfer, already approved by the signature at the bottom: BJ Abbott.

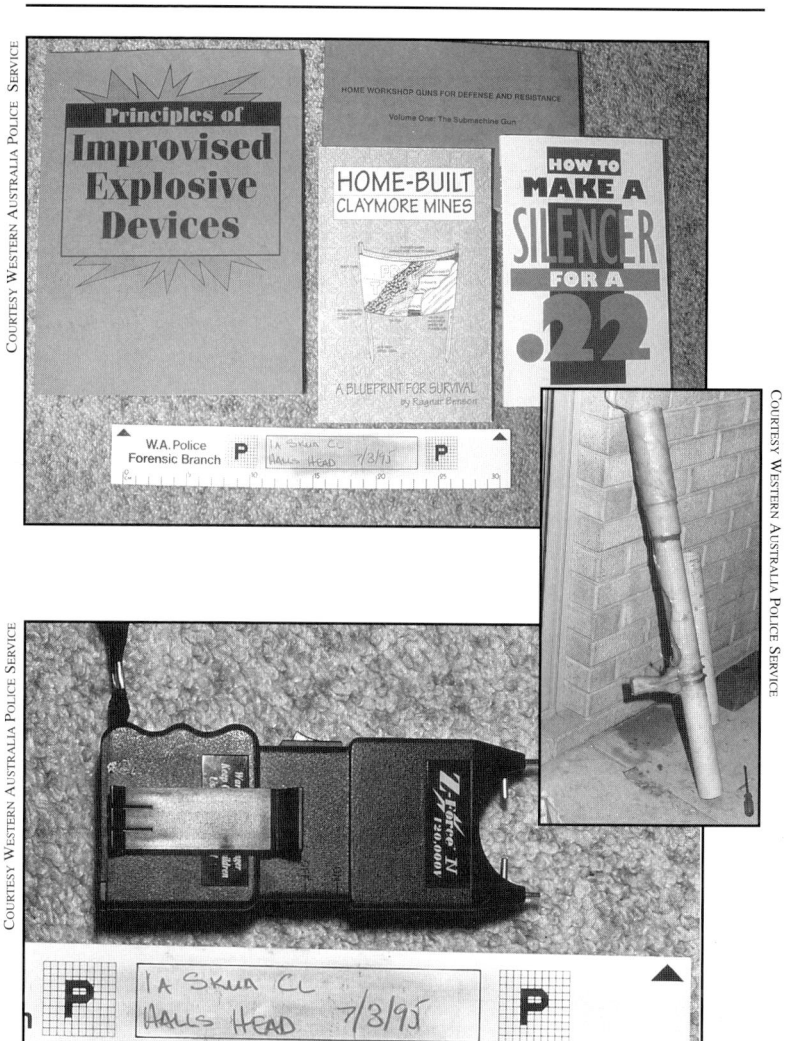

Principles of **Improvised Explosive Devices**

HOME-BUILT CLAYMORE MINES

A BLUEPRINT FOR SURVIVAL
by Ragnar Benson

HOME WORKSHOP GUNS FOR DEFENSE AND RESISTANCE
Volume One: The Submachine Gun

HOW TO MAKE A SILENCER FOR A .22

When WA police raided Glenn Abbott's home south of Perth in March 1995, they uncovered a full-blown criminal operation which supported his brother's activities on the other side of the country. The haul included a criminal 'library' (top), a homemade rocket launcher (right), and a 120,000 volt taser (bottom), which Glenn admitted had 'put him on the ground for half an hour' when he tested it on himself.

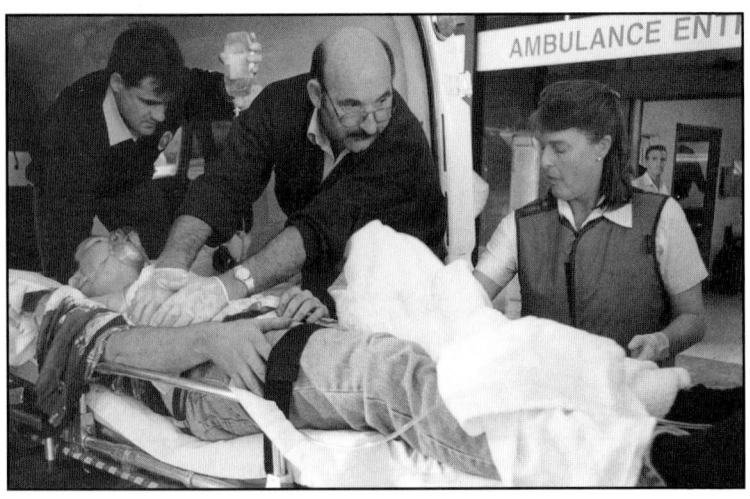

Kelly Fisher, outside a Perth court in 1998. She told *The West Australian* that her de facto husband, Glenn Abbott, was being victimised because of his brother's crimes.

'I'm a criminal, mate, not a killer. I didn't mean to. I was pressured into it.' Ambulance officers rush Glenn Abbott into Royal Perth Hospital in September, 1996. He was critically injured in a gun battle with a police officer who was trying to issue a speeding ticket.

Special Tactics and Rescue Division officers approach a National Australia Bank branch in Adelaide on 1 December, 1997. It was typical of the response to noises in bank ceilings while Abbott was on the run.

Abbott 'apprentice' Brendan Berichon was in awe of Abbott when they met in the Sir David Longland Correctional Centre.

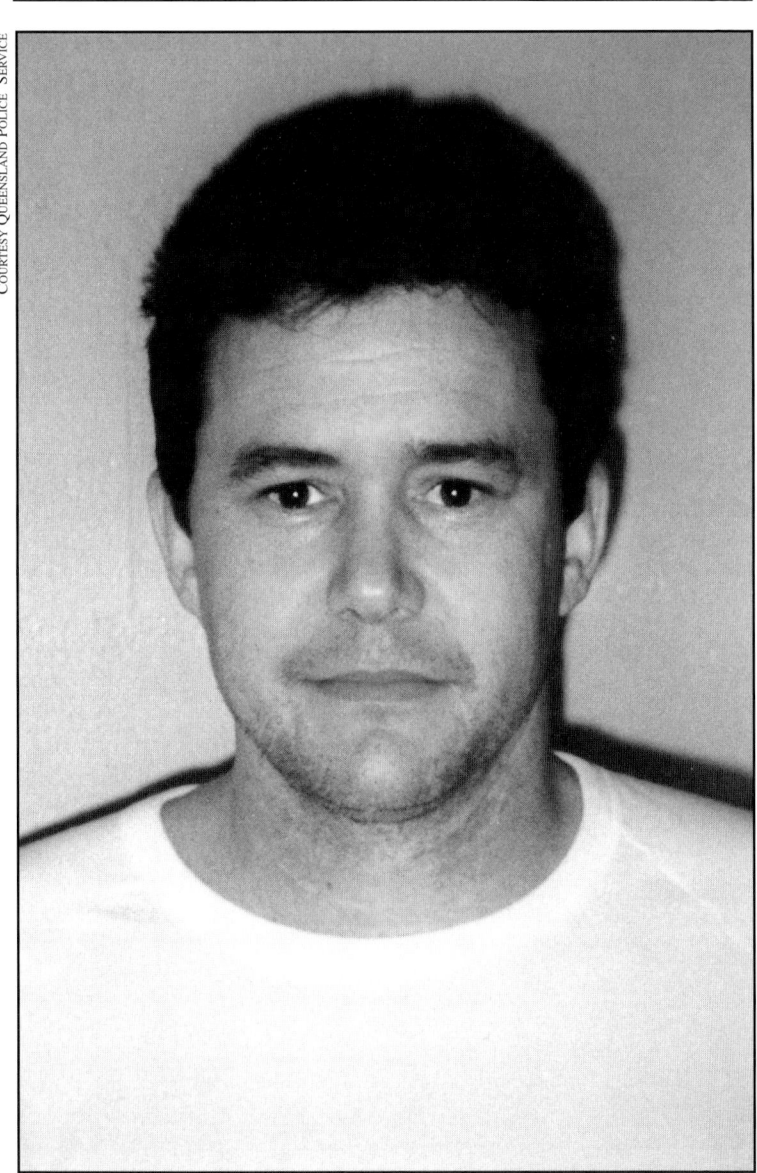

Abbott in custody in Queensland in the 1990s.

Special Emergency Response Team officers search bushland at Forest Lake in Brisbane in the wake of the Sir David Longland escape.

Abbott was returning to this Darwin laundry when Territory Response Group officers swooped in May, 1998.

Once such a mystery to investigators, Abbott's face became a regular sight in newspapers and on television. His Darwin recapture attracted national headlines.

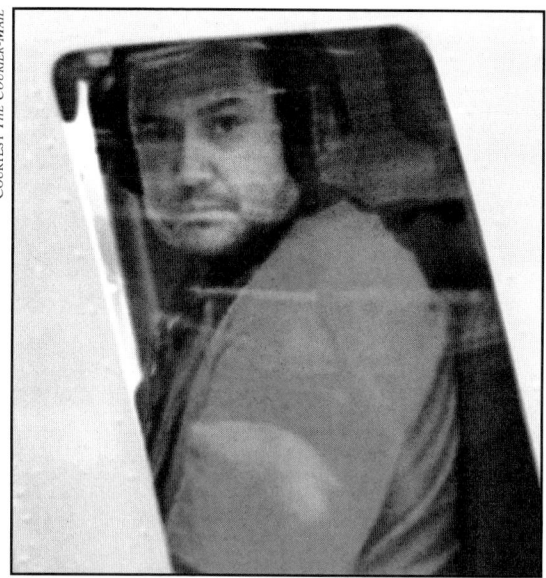

Abbott glares from a helicopter window on his way to Woodford Prison, after being returned to Brisbane from Darwin on a government jet.

Brendan Berichon is driven from the Luma Luma Apartments in Darwin after his peaceful surrender.

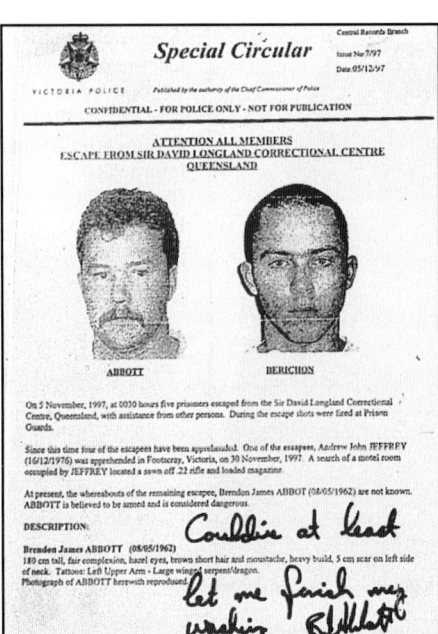

'Could've at least let me finish my washing. BJ Abbott.' Detectives from around the nation flew to Darwin to question Abbott, but he was offering nothing more than autographs.

While Abbott was on the run, authorities allowed media to photograph the special cell they had prepared for him at Woodford Prison's maximum security unit.

Chapter 15

City under siege

'*We consider these five escapees to be the most dangerous and desperate people on the streets of Australia at the moment and police are . . . terrified as to what they may do to stay at large.*'
— Queensland Police media spokesman Brian Swift, Brisbane, 5 November 1997

The prison's understaffing problems had provided the perfect window for final preparations on Melbourne Cup day, 1997. For six and a half hours earlier that day, Unit 4B had been locked down, with the prisoners confined to cells. It was a security measure used whenever prison staff numbers fell short — a regular occurrence at Sir David Longland.

But the rules allowed for the unit cook, Garry Merrick, to continue with his duties, and he was subject only to cursory patrols by guards. Merrick — whose girlfriend had helped smuggle in the angel wire — is believed to have heated up a metal-handled serving utensil in the unit's kitchen to use as a melting tool.

The backs were removed from plastic chairs to form the crude

block's razor wire perimeter with the modified chair parts.

Sprinting towards the three perimeter fences, they were spotted just after midnight and the alarm was raised by the on-duty officer in the prison's security control room. But he was only relieving in the position, and wasn't aware of the direct-line 000 facility at his fingertips. He eventually tried the number after getting no answer at the local police station.

Meanwhile, three of the ten prison officers on duty that night had begun running towards the inmates, who had gathered near the first inner perimeter fence. One later described the scene as 'like a war'.

'There were heaps of shots. It was all a big haze,' he would later tell a court.

In between the shots came a blunt warning from one of the inmates. 'Stay down, you cunts, or you'll go down.' Unarmed and without radios, the officers heeded the warning and took cover.

A perimeter security camera captured the five as all hell broke loose around them. They looked relaxed and unhurried as boltcutters and a gun with silencer were heaved over the three fences. But the gun dropped short of the innermost fence, and was left behind in the rush to get out. The boltcutters were retrieved, and, with Abbott directing the shots, they spent the next six minutes working their way through the three fences.

There were no signs of concern as the prison's armoured vehicle rumbled around the perimeter corner. Its arrival had been expected. The first of close to a dozen shots suddenly rang out, with the distinctive crack of a high-calibre weapon. Both batteries were struck, stopping the vehicle in its tracks.

Prison officer Mark Fritz felt a piece of debris strike as he went in search of a weapon in the rear of the vehicle. But with the vehicle disabled and the gun portals on the side pointing in the wrong direction, he and driver Mark Irvin were left trapped and helpless for close to 25 minutes.

One of the outside accomplice or accomplices — up to three are believed to have been involved — then helped the escapees overcome the outer razor-topped fence. The area was surrounded by scrubland, providing good cover as the group ran to the waiting getaway car and sped off down a back road.

Police had now begun to respond to the escape alert, and a patrol car soon spotted a white Ford Fairlane speeding across the Ipswich Road overpass at Wacol. They gave chase, but hurriedly dropped back when one of the occupants leaned out the window and delivered a volley of shots. Just after 1 am, a private security officer on patrol in the nearby suburb of Forest Lake approached a car parked at the end of a cul de sac with its lights turned on. He was also forced to beat a hasty retreat as more shots rang out and the car sped off. A few minutes later, police found the car abandoned in a small park, with ammunition strewn across its blood-soaked seats.

Now, the hunt would begin in earnest.

The nervousness had set in the night before, with constant sirens and helicopters alerting a large part of Brisbane that something was seriously amiss. The endless bulletins on the morning radio and the presence of heavily armed police on the streets confirmed it. The city set about its day with a sense of caution and fear. It seemed that anything could happen next. The rest of the nation watched, intrigued, unaware that the shockwaves of the night's events would later spread to several other states.

The escape was unprecedented in recent Australian history, and the response from the Queensland Police was immediate and massive. Hundreds of officers scoured the city's streets in the following 48 hours, and a special operation, Korn, was formed to coordinate what developed into a massive logistical exercise. In the back of each officer's mind was the unhesitating use of extreme violence the previous night. The task they now faced was unenviable. While recapture was paramount, their urgency had to be balanced against the need for caution. If one of the escapees were cornered, or an unprepared police patrol should stumble on them, the outcome could be disastrous.

Each new tip and scrap of intelligence was investigated vigilantly, and grave warnings were issued to the public. 'We consider these five escapees to be the most dangerous and desperate people on the streets of Australia at the moment and police are absolutely petrified and terrified as to what they may do to stay at large,' police media spokesman Brian Swift announced.

Residents were told to travel in pairs or, preferably, to stay at home behind locked doors. Fears that the escapees may have staged a home invasion to secure a temporary safe house also prompted police advice to check on friends and relatives regularly.

The overnight search had continued to focus on Forest Lake and the surrounding south-western suburbs that day, and a section of the area was cordoned off following a report that Nixon, Stirling and Jeffrey had been seen fleeing into bushland. Just before 2.30 pm, a man bought clothing, tape, sunglasses, chocolate and a bag from the nearby Big W supermarket at Mt Ommaney and returned to the Forest Lake area.

The trio who had been sighted had been hiding out in a bush shelter in the area. After changing into the new clothes, they moved on, leaving behind a semi-automatic rifle, ammunition, prison uniforms, unopened packets of new clothes and the Big W receipt. At this point, their plans seemed to lose direction, with their next move sparking high drama in the city's afternoon peak hour rush. About mid-afternoon they set out on foot in search of transport, emerging from scrubland in Carole Park. The trio spoke briefly, and then Peter Stirling walked over to the front yard of a nearby house, where 19-year-old Brad Schofield was working on his car. Stirling asked if he could call them a cab.

'No problem,' the young man replied. 'Just wait here while I go inside.' They followed him in, taking the chance to raid the fridge for drinks, tend to minor wounds, and eat before the cab arrived.

The car from Yellow Cabs arrived a few minutes later and they began heading towards the city. Meanwhile, police had been

area, believing they had them trapped. Diners in nearby cafes and restaurants were locked in as the search continued, but after several hours the operation was scaled back and the waiting game recommenced.

As Abbott had planned, his fellow escapees had captured the full attention of the police. Brenden, of whom there was no sign, had slipped away to plan his next move.

The seriousness of the escape and the threat it posed to the community made it an immediate political issue. The state's prison system had been plagued with escapes, and the Opposition was now calling for the head of Prisons Minister Russell Cooper. He responded by promising massive security upgrades. Australia, he said, had begun a new era of criminal violence and Queensland would be the first to fight back. He also promised a 'no holds barred' inquiry, and former Drugs in Prison Commissioner Carl Mengler from Victoria was appointed to head a team of five prison inspectors.

Several weeks later they delivered a far-reaching report, highlighting serious deficiencies in the prison's security and recommending an overhaul of the state's prison system which would cost tens of millions of dollars. The inspectors paid particular attention to Abbott in their report, acknowledging his role as the organiser but showing clear annoyance with his image. They wrote:

> *A lot of publicity has been given to this event by the media and the five inmates who escaped in this instance have received some kudos.*
>
> *It has been said the escapee Abbott is of high intellect and a master of planning which added to the success of this venture, when in the view of the inspectors this is not the case. This escape by the five inmates is nothing more than a basic operation [and] did not require the planning skills of a mastermind.*
>
> *The ingredients required to make this operation successful were little more than the desire and motivation to escape, the ability to observe the existing conditions, the contacts to obtain basic tools and assistance and preparedness to take the risk.*

But it wasn't that simple, and they knew it. Certainly, it had taken more than Abbott's skills alone for it to succeed — the report summed up the prison's response as substandard, with poor coordination, inadequate training and ineffective leadership all contributing to the success of the escape.

However, it does not necessarily follow that an escape attempt of this magnitude could have been prevented by the centre staff in isolation,' the inspectors admitted. 'In the six and a half to seven minutes that transpired after the alarm, given all circumstances, there was little more that any of the officers could have done.'

So where was Abbott now? Fuelled by tales he had told other inmates, rumours and speculation about his plans spread quickly. From Broome and Darwin to Indonesia and South America, there was a destination to match each theory, usually involving the inevitable stories of Abbott's 'buried treasure'.

His options seemed limitless. Perth, Alice Springs, Darwin, Adelaide, Melbourne, Sydney, north-west Western Australia, northern Queensland, Tasmania — there were few places he hadn't been in his travels.

And somewhere, probably in some far-flung regional town or city, there had to be a storage shed. Abbott was a great believer in preparing for the future, as the sheds found previously on the Gold Coast and in Cairns and Perth had demonstrated. With guns, money and tools of trade at his fingertips, anything could happen — but first he had to get to it.

On November 13, Abbott is alleged to have joined forces with Jason Nixon and robbed the Commonwealth Bank in Palm Beach, on the Gold Coast. He'd already faced charges over an elaborate robbery at the branch in 1993, but the latest operation was straight to the point.

Nixon, who was later convicted of the robbery, stood by with a tomahawk and looked menacing while his accomplice ordered the staff to fill two shopping bags with cash. 'We don't want to hurt you. This is our way of making a living,' he assured them. They escaped with about $17 000. Travelling money, detectives theorised. Where would Abbott turn up next?

It had become a frequently asked question, and the Queensland Labor Party would make it a focus of their campaign for the state election the following year. Some 150 000 leaflets bearing the question 'Where is Brendon [sic] Abbott?' were distributed, embarrassing the government and increasing the pressure on police to recapture him. As it was, they had thrown every available resource into the investigation, which was being run from a major incident room at police headquarters in Brisbane.

The operation was overseen by Detective Superintendent Kerry Dunn, and an individual detective was assigned to each escapee, and later, Brendan Berichon. Security around the operation was tight and it was made clear from the start that leaks could not be allowed to compromise the investigation. As a result, the release of information to interstate detectives was again limited, prompting some to lament that they hadn't learned from the mistakes of the past.

Probe: Flanders had proved in 1995 that a national approach was the most effective method of hunting Abbott. After five years of free rein, they had recaptured him within just six months. Now, most states had reactivated their Abbott investigations, but were working as separate entities.

Sid Thomas, who headed Operation Hiker in Adelaide, would be kept occupied over the next few months with surveillance operations and a flurry of reported sightings. Across the nation, there would be hundreds, and combined with a big increase in

Chapter 16

Sex, drugs and stupidity

> *'Blessed be the truly unwise, for they bring hope to those obligated to pursue them.'*
> — David Simon,
> *Homicide — A Year on the Killing Streets*

Back on the east coast, the other four escapees had performed admirably in their role as decoys. But as calculating fugitives, they failed spectacularly.

In the days after three of them had slipped through the net in the city, Operation Korn raided address after address in a highly publicised assault on the Queensland criminal community. They were determined to uncover the escapees and it was made clear that close scrutiny would continue until they turned up. Anyone thinking about aiding them was well-advised to think twice. As well, their faces and names were firmly imprinted in the minds of the public, who were offering tips and sightings across the state.

With so many eyes and ears on alert, it made sense to take a leaf out of Abbott's book and lay low. But rapist Peter Stirling couldn't help himself and soon became a victim of his appetites. He visited a brothel at Tweed Heads, just over the border in New South Wales, two nights after the escape. While he drove a prostitute to a house at Mermaid Beach back across the border, her worried co-workers were contacting police, believing they had recognised him.

The house was surrounded and after a short phone conversation, Stirling surrendered just after dawn. In escaping, he had risked life, limb and a further lengthy jail term. The net return of two days of freedom and a night of sex hardly seemed worth it.

The recapture set the tone for his colleagues, with Oliver Alincic succumbing to similar desires a few days later. He'd struck out on his own, driving a stolen car to the northern New South Wales town of Nimbin in search of drugs and sex. Scoring marijuana in the town was no great challenge, but Alincic's idea of romance soon caused trouble.

He'd met another young man since arriving, and on November 11, he decided to test the short friendship by propositioning his girlfriend. When the drugs-for-sex offer was refused, Alincic chased the young girl down the street. She found her boyfriend, who was about to set him straight when Alincic pulled a pistol and drove off in a hurry.

The pair reported Alincic to police, who found him at a local service station three hours later, oblivious to the fuss he had caused. Alincic tried to flee through the rear of the service station, but was quickly cornered and arrested. After facing a local court, where his offences in the town were quickly dealt with, an application was granted for immediate extradition. A helicopter ride and armed convoy later, Alincic was back behind bars in Queensland.

Nine days later, flush with robbery proceeds, Jason Nixon was found living it up at a luxury resort in Noosa, on the Sunshine Coast, with a female companion. But the detectives who came knocking on the door weren't even looking for him — they were there on a drug warrant. Nixon, who was armed, managed to let a shot go before the stunned officers tackled him to the ground.

Later, after imposing an 18-year sentence and declaring Nixon a serious violent offender, Brisbane District Court Judge Fred McGuire mused over why men such as Abbott and Nixon had fallen through the cracks. Both had been criminally inclined from an early age, but the system, the judge said, had failed to help them.

'Experience — bitter experience — has shown that many career criminals, such as Abbott and Nixon, started out as juvenile delinquents and for one reason or another, the system — the social, police and judicial system — could not adequately deal with these offenders and it has developed into monumental offending over the years,' he said.

Abbott, at least, could lay claim to indifferent treatment in his youth — notably his first lengthy stint in a juvenile detention centre and the harshness of Fremantle Prison. But he had long since abandoned the old chestnut of a tough childhood to justify his actions. From the moment he had slipped out the back door of Nollamara CIB in 1987, Abbott had been a professional fugitive and criminal — and he took pride in it. It was a career, of sorts, which required specialised skills and a ruthless attitude, and was governed by a curious code of ethics.

Jason Nixon, on the other hand, had few skills and followed no rules. His taste for casual violence had made him one of the

would prove that Jeffrey could make no such claim.

In search of alcohol and trouble, he embarked on a night of bumbleheaded drunkenness which would later be immortalised by investigative reporters Gary Tippet and John Silvester, in a *Sunday Age* article, appropriately entitled 'Dumb and Dumber'. It was a tale of two bar flies, a 'knucklehead' and a sick cop in the right place at the right time.

Well-primed, Jeffrey had adjourned to the Royal Hotel for the evening, where his boozy boasts of murder and robbery soon annoyed two men watching TV at the bar. He had more jobs planned, he told them. He just needed someone to pinch a car for him. The men, 'Garry' and 'Garry's mate', incredulous at how the situation then unfolded, later related the night's events to the reporters.

'Mate, you reckon you're such a good crook, you can go nick one yourself,' was Garry's mate's terse response to Jeffrey's proposition. But half-full and fired up, Jeffrey, who was calling himself Peter, wouldn't leave it alone. He was a famous and dangerous prison escapee, dammit. He wanted some respect. But still, they refused to believe him.

'I mean, who's going to believe someone when they say something like that?' Garry told the *Sunday Age*. 'Anybody in their right fucking mind, they'd keep it quiet, wouldn't they?'

Not Jeffrey. Tempers became frayed and fingers were pointed, until Garry called for a truce. He left with his mate soon after, and they parted ways. A few minutes later, Jeffrey suddenly grabbed Garry from behind on the street, demanding to know where his mate had gone. But he didn't know, and when Jeffrey began pushing him down the street to look, Garry decided enough was enough. Pulling him to the ground, he made a final effort to convince Jeffrey to walk away. 'Peter, I haven't done anything to you, just leave me alone.'

But after helping him to his feet, the drunken temper which had already made Jeffrey a killer suddenly resurfaced. Garry went down under a barrage of punches, and his memory is hazy about what happened after he hit the ground. 'But I remember this part: He said, "I'm gonna find an alleyway and then you're a dead man". That's when I finally twigged this wasn't just some pub brawl. He'd been telling the truth and I really was a dead man.' The realisation made Garry all the more grateful for the next turn of events.

Constable Andy Logan, attached to the Werribee Traffic Section, was stopped at a red light nearby when he noticed the attack in progress. He'd been fighting the flu all week and had elected to head home for the night, having just pulled over to recover from a lengthy coughing fit. But the guy on the ground was copping a hiding. He couldn't ignore it.

Logan quickly catching up on foot and twisting his arm behind his back. Jeffrey turned and prepared to unload a punch with his right hand, but the officer twisted harder, bringing him to the ground and quickly slipping the cuffs in place. Logan sat on Jeffrey's back and struggled to catch his breath, while a bruised and battered Garry told him about the escapee's unlikely tale.

Back at the station, the reaction was sceptical. Could one of the nation's most wanted men have publicly announced his identity and then bashed a man in the street for not believing him? Surely not. But it didn't take long to confirm.

Jeffrey faced Melbourne Magistrates Court the next day on assault and firearms charges, after a rifle was recovered from his motel room. A four-month suspended jail term was immediately imposed when he pleaded guilty, and extradition proceedings commenced soon after.

Queensland Police spokesman Brian Swift expressed relief that four of the escapees had now been recaptured. 'It doesn't matter how they've been caught, the fact is they're behind bars and can commit no further offences,' he said.

But he warned that the remaining escapee would be tougher to catch. 'It doesn't appear Abbott's quite that stupid,' he said, adding that 100 officers would continue to work on the case. 'The intelligence base and the database is growing daily . . . and that's increasing our chances of getting him. He's shown a reasonable amount of intelligence so far in staying away, but the fact is that last time Abbott was out he did make a mistake and he did get caught. It just took some time. This time, if he makes another mistake, police somewhere in Australia will be ready to get him.'

Investigations into the breakout had also provided another target for detectives. On November 12, police announced that Berichon was believed to be travelling with Abbott. 'He has a fascination for Abbott and his notoriety. We are very concerned. He's a young fellow and he may be led up the garden path,' Brian Swift told the media.

Detectives were well aware that Berichon's drug use conflicted with Abbott's philosophies and operating methods. There was no telling what might happen, and the concern for his safety prompted Julie Berichon to make a public appeal to her son. Maybe, the detectives hoped, he would listen to his mother.

'Brendan, give yourself up. Please come home. We love you. We don't want you getting into any more trouble,' she said during an emotional news conference with her daughter, Linda, by her side. He was in way over his head, his sister said, and should just give himself up.

But if he heard his family's pleas, Berichon ignored them. Being on the run with Australia's most wanted man carried a lot of appeal, and he didn't share the concerns for his safety.

Speculation would grow in the next few months over the nature of his relationship with Abbott, with suggestions that they were more than good friends. Trusting a known drug user was uncharacteristic and risky. Sex seemed the only remote but plausible explanation. But by the following year, it would become clear that the two had forged a different sort of bond.

Berichon's loyalty was rivalled only by Glenn Abbott's intense and dangerous devotion, and he was already alleged to have put his life — and others — on the line for the sake of his mentor's freedom. Abbott owed him and knew it, returning the loyalty in spite of the potential risks. He'd worked with and

police units around the country grew weary of high-tension callouts which always seemed to end in anticlimax.

An incident on a Sydney street in November was typical. Abbott was at a Thai Airways office queuing for a ticket, according to the tip. After the street was quickly evacuated, police descended on a group of people they had been led to believe contained Abbott. Instead, they found a bemused model, make-up artist and camera crew who had been conducting a magazine fashion shoot, oblivious to the drama.

Sid Thomas was experiencing similar frustrations in Adelaide. Intelligence and reliable sightings by people who knew Abbott had convinced him the escapee had been in the city in late November. Nothing concrete had resulted, but then, early on December 1, suspicions heightened again when a city bank employee arrived for work to find an alarm ringing and two ceiling tiles missing. The area around the National Australia branch in Hutt Street was cordoned off and a team of heavily armed STAR Division officers moved in behind armoured shields.

Within a few days, yet another new theory surfaced that Abbott was laying low in Victoria with Berichon. It made sense — without the warrants, suspicions and political pressure which motivated other states, Victorian Police had no pressing reason to commit resources to an active search. It was a crucial, but less obvious, consideration which would appeal to Abbott's security-conscious nature. As it was, his current circumstances were already demanding a special level of vigilance and caution. And he was well aware that the price on his head was now substantial, and could encourage those outside the boundaries of law enforcement to join the hunt.

Initially, the Queensland state government and Australian Bankers Association (ABA) had each offered a $50 000 reward. On December 9, ABA spokesman Kevin Broadribb announced that the association had doubled its offer to $100 000, on the advice of police. But the high level of fear Abbott was generating in the banking sector no doubt played a part in the decision —

first class during an inflight encounter with another Australian celebrity, journalist Jana Wendt. Abbott had apparently boasted about the incident, and newspaper gossip columns loved the story's ironical twist. Wendt had been under fire from the media over Uncensored, her $1.1 million series for the ABC which featured interviews with prominent figures in society. Abbott — the nation's most wanted man and interview subject — sat next to her and struck up a conversation. But she didn't seem to recognise him, and when the Melbourne-bound flight touched down, the chance for a ratings winner passed by.

Theories that he was laying low in Victoria gained strength on December 19, when a report put him at Melbourne Airport at 6 am, about to board a flight to Brisbane. He was a well-known frequent flyer and the response from airport security and federal and state police was immediate and dramatic. As flak-jacketed officers swarmed through the terminal and word spread that they were hunting for Abbott, fear quickly spread among commuters. The passenger who made the report believed he had seen Abbott walking through the departure area, and Qantas delayed flights until a thorough search was completed. But when the man who had been sighted was found, it turned out to be the usual case of mistaken identity.

Then, just a few hours later on the other side of the country, came yet another promising sighting. And this time, there was no mistake.

Chapter 17

Home again

*'We really didn't expect him to come here straight away.
That would be too obvious.'*

— Detective Sergeant Jack Lee,
Perth Armed Robbery Squad

Perth had been a long way from the action this time, but distance hadn't dulled the city's fear of, and fascination with, Brenden Abbott. Police and banks in Western Australia knew better than anyone that he could reappear anywhere at any time, and false alarms and sightings had been plentiful in the weeks after the escape.

'We really didn't expect him to come here straight away. That would be too obvious,' Detective Sergeant Jack Lee says. Even so, nothing was left to chance. The entire Armed Robbery Squad had initially been involved in the operation, interviewing old associates, executing search warrants, arranging surveillance and following up leads.

In one particularly secretive operation, the funeral of Abbott's grandmother was kept under surveillance, and it is believed

standing outside the Mirrabooka branch of the Commonwealth Bank. Some staff members even commented on his odd appearance when they arrived for work on December 19, but more out of humour than suspicion. The business suit and briefcase seemed normal enough, but the grey hair and moustache were less than convincing. He'd been standing outside watching them arrive since 8.30 am, waiting for the right moment.

As usual, Abbott had done his homework on staff numbers, and it was later estimated that the job had taken about a week to set up. When a female bank officer approached the front door at 8.50 am, he made his move, pressing a gun to her neck and following her inside. Moving quickly, he ordered the dozen or so staff members up against a wall before they had a chance to activate cameras or alarms.

Throughout the robbery, he held what some staff thought was a scanner or two-way radio to his ear. But the manager, whom Abbott had immediately focused on, was sure it was a mobile phone. Within a few minutes, the treasury time locks released and he quickly cleaned it out.

There were reports of a young man standing inside the bank's doorway during the robbery, but with the staff traumatised and facing the wall for most of the incident, it was difficult to confirm. It was initially thought he may have been a customer, but another unconfirmed report put him inside the bank carrying a bag during the robbery.

Eight minutes after he entered the bank, the bandit bolted out the front door after ordering staff into the toilet. Media reports put the haul at $450 000, but detectives say it was closer to a third of a million. The bandit was sighted by several people as he left the bank and when they were later shown photoboards by police, four witnesses pointed to Abbott's picture.

The flimsy disguise had achieved its purpose of getting him inside, but Abbott knew anything more sophisticated was a waste of time — he'd be a suspect anyway, probably before the first

As evidence went, it didn't get any better — particularly in the age of DNA testing — and the sweat and skin residue from the disguise would conclusively prove the wearer's identity. Once before, it had led to Abbott's downfall — the blood smear from the Eleanora robbery in 1996 — when even the best efforts of his defence team couldn't undermine its reliability.

After a six-week search, the blood sample from that case was finally tracked down in Queensland, and a comparison with the samples from the disguise put the chances of Abbott not being the wearer at one in 45 million.

But while the evidence was strong, the suspect remained elusive. Five detectives and two analysts were working full-time on the case, and in the days after the robbery, airports around the country — particularly Perth — were closely watched. But he'd left the same day as the robbery, dumping a Mazda at the airport as a decoy and then heading south-east out of the city in a green Toyota LandCruiser.

After staying overnight in Albany, Abbott hit the road again, reaching Alice Springs on Christmas Eve. The same day, a call to police in Kalgoorlie — where old foe Jeff Beaman was based — claimed Abbott was about to rob a bank in the nearby town of Norseman — a town he would have passed through in the previous couple of days.

A few weeks later at the Perth Skyshow, a public announcement for Brenden Abbott to report to the Police Post drew laughs from the crowd. But the jocular attitude of the public wore thin with detectives, and in March, when a woman claimed to have spent a night with Abbott in the Perth Hyatt, she was charged with making a false report.

There were positive leads, though. Intelligence had thrown up the name of Gary Anderson, another former associate from Abbott's Fremantle days who had been linked to his current activities. Anderson had absconded while on bail for armed robbery in Queensland, and was now believed to be in Perth. A week-long search failed to find any trace of him, until another stroke of luck occurred on January 21.

Anderson had been involved in a car accident, and when Kelly Fisher — still under close police scrutiny — went to pick him up from a Midland panelbeater, there was a surveillance team in tow. They were trailed north to the Yanchep Holiday Village, where Anderson was arrested a few hours later.

'We brought him back and interviewed him, but he was no different to Abbott. They're old-style crims who won't give you any grief, but won't say a thing about what they've done,' Jack Lee says.

Even the friendly approach failed. 'Give me a statement so that I can get a trip to Queensland for your trial,' one detective said to Anderson.

Glenn Abbott was now on another attempted murder charge over an incident at Casuarina Prison in 1997, while on remand over the shooting of police officer Lee Watson. He appeared in court on January 28 to face a preliminary hearing, amid the type of security operation normally reserved for his brother. With the Tactical Response Group hovering outside, he stood in the dock shackled and surrounded by guards.

When Magistrate Paul Heaney refused Abbott's lawyer's requests for the chains to be removed and the proceedings suppressed, Glenn exploded with rage. 'This is just bullshit. You guys can just kiss my arse. I ain't going to sit here quietly,' he shouted. 'You turn around and victimise me for someone else's actions. Why don't you just get on with screwing me?'

After one adjournment, the magistrate became tired of the chain-rattling and ejected Abbott before continuing the proceedings. His alleged victim, another inmate, testified that Abbott had approached him in prison on July 24 the previous year and asked to 'have a yarn'. He'd never met Abbott and was wary when he sat down a few feet away from him.

'He said to me: "My name is Abbott, I heard you've got someone out to kill me",' the inmate told the court.

'I said: "Bullshit, I don't even know you. Why would I want to kill you?" Then within a second he pulled something out of his pocket and swung me around . . . and there was a jab directly under my jaw.'

Two lengthy scars on his neck were testament to his injuries. After the evidence was outlined, the magistrate committed Abbott to trial. He later pleaded guilty.

Outside court, Kelly Fisher vented her anger at the treatment of Abbott in an interview with *The West Australian*, saying Glenn was being victimised because of his brother. Rumours that Brenden would try to break him out were a joke, she said, because he didn't care about his family. 'He's living his own life — why would he bother?' she told the paper. 'Glenn's already guilty in the eyes of the public. It's disgusting — he sat in court with shackles on. Why did he have to have those on? They didn't give him a chance.'

But police made no apologies for the security measures. An escape attempt involving his brother may have seemed far-fetched, but no more so than the Sir David Longland escape.

In fact, Brenden Abbott was long gone. With money in his pocket and a new base selected on the other side of the country, it was time to lay low again.

Chapter 18

The price of loyalty

*'He made no threats, gave no warning. He just pulled
the gun out, cocked it, pointed it at me and began to fire.'*
— Senior Constable Peter Baltas, describing
Brendan Berichon's reaction to being stopped
in a Melbourne street on 20 April 1998

From the outside, it looked perfect. There were four terrace
cottages in the group, which faced Nicholson Street, a busy
Carlton thoroughfare not far from the heart of Melbourne. But if
they wanted to, the residents could easily avoid the noisy traffic
and constant flow of pedestrians past their front doors. The small
courtyards out the back provided easy rear access, opening on to
a laneway just metres from a quiet side street.

Lena Paplos — next door at No. 43 — noticed that the two
men at No. 41 always used it in preference to the front entrance.
The older man, who had bought a four-wheel drive since
arriving, would park it in the side street and slip in through the
back roller door. With his black Akubra, sunglasses, moustache
and casual but expensive clothes, he looked quite the part.
Probably a businessman, she thought. He arrived a few weeks

after the younger one, who had kept a very low profile since moving in about mid-January 1998.

'I thought we had the perfect neighbours,' she says. 'They never complained about our music and always minded their own business. Even the landlord said they were really cool.'

Brendan Berichon had been nervy when he answered the newspaper ad and first arrived to look at the place, but not enough to arouse suspicion. His clothes were casual but neat, and the baseball cap, glasses and timid manner gave him a particularly boyish look. The owners liked him — and the roll of cash he offered to cover the first four months' rent. Another mate would be moving in soon, he told them, and they would both be looking for jobs. Over the next few months, they became ideal but unremarkable tenants and neighbours. Once again, Abbott had found safety in suburban anonymity.

But throughout the early part of 1998, it seemed that something convinced local detectives the pair were in Melbourne. Abbott certainly had links to the city. His father, long gone but never forgotten, had been living in west suburban St Albans until the media attention forced him to move. Over the years, there were rumours that Abbott had maintained contact — a part of him perhaps still wanting to believe the tales of his father being a big-time crook.

As well as the family link to Melbourne, detectives had been looking closely at local armed robberies. In particular, they are believed to have focused on a robbery in Dandenong on March 13, in which two Armaguard employees were relieved of $250 000 by two men. It didn't seem to be Abbott's style, and he would later vehemently deny involvement. But at the time, anything seemed possible.

rack and, when Abbott settled on the right one, a new V8 engine. Soon, it would be a camper's dream.

But unforeseen events would force the project to be abandoned before the new motor could be fitted. Brendan Berichon, so reliable and useful up to this point, had earned

Abbott's trust and gratitude. Now, he had resumed his heroin habit with gusto. And loyalty to a drug user, as Abbott would soon discover, came at a high price.

Berichon had wasted no time in making a contact in the Melbourne drug scene, approaching a teenage street kid in the city. They came to an arrangement which would become routine — the kid scored, Berichon paid and they shared the drugs.

But a police crackdown on street dealing in the city forced a change of plan, and on April 20 the pair headed to the east suburban Box Hill Central shopping centre. They soon found what they were looking for but, as the deal went down, two passing transit police officers took an interest in the proceedings.

When Berichon and his mate fled into the crowds of mid-afternoon shoppers, Sergeant Scott Roberts and Senior Constable Peter Baltas gave chase, and a patrol of the area soon turned them up in nearby Surrey Drive.

It was routine enough. Baltas questioned Berichon, while his partner approached the teenager. Berichon began fumbling inside a bum bag when Baltas asked for identification, and then produced a false Queensland driver's licence. But he rushed it, and the officer caught a glimpse of the large roll of cash inside. Panicking, Berichon reached in again, and from that moment on, Baltas would later tell a court, the incident seemed to pass in slow motion.

'As he was questioned, he pulled the gun out of the bum bag. I heard several shots in rapid succession and my body spun towards the car,' he said. 'I can remember feeling as though this could not be happening to me. There was blood on my clothing

shots from the nine-millimetre pistol. Baltas, at point blank range, should have been dead. But Berichon's aim was wild, and the officer was only hit twice — in the leg and hip — before managing to dive behind the patrol car.

'I'm probably one of the luckiest in the world, I suppose. We both are,' he said after being released from hospital a few days later.

Scott Roberts, standing about three metres away, took one bullet in the arm before managing to draw his weapon and return fire.

'I wasn't trying to kill them,' Berichon would later tell police. But they were Victorian coppers. He believed it was a case of shoot or be shot.

When the wounded sergeant began firing, Berichon turned and sprinted off, jumping one fence and then scaling a cyclone fence topped with barbed wire. His young mate also bolted, wanting no part in a gun battle.

In a blind panic, Berichon ran up to a house where a woman visiting an elderly friend was standing at the front door. 'He was pointing a weapon at me a couple of feet away, at my chest area,' the 54-year-old later told Melbourne Magistrates Court. 'He said: "Come quickly, I have to get out of here, I have to go to the city. I'll direct you. Just do what I say and you won't get hurt".' He grabbed her arm and began guiding her towards her car.

Scott Roberts, meanwhile, had radioed for back-up and after being treated by paramedics, the officers were rushed to a local hospital. They were soon reported to be in a satisfactory condition, which was welcome news to the huge contingent of officers which had saturated the area around the shooting. Nothing brought a swifter response than a report of two members down with gunshot wounds — especially as the memories of Walsh Street still rankled. In October 1988, Constables Steven Tynan and Damian Eyre had been gunned down in the South Yarra street while responding to an early morning report of an abandoned vehicle. It was an alleged payback over the shooting of a criminal a few hours before, and had remained a source of pain for many — including Scott Roberts, who had been a mate of Tynan's.

Now, as news of the latest shooting spread, detectives, beat officers, patrol cars, dogs and helicopters began scouring the city, in a massive operation which would be coordinated by the Special Response Squad.

Berichon, directing his reluctant chauffeur across the city, was aware of the urgent need to get out of the area and became frustrated as the late afternoon traffic slowed their progress. But it was important to keep a grip — the woman was terrified, and she might attract someone's attention or have an accident if he didn't keep her calm. He kept reassuring her that she would be released as soon as they reached Carlton, and made small talk about his family and football to take her mind off the situation.

'Do you follow the footy? I'm a North Melbourne fan.' In an equally conversational tone, he mentioned he'd shot two police officers and was 'in trouble'.

After almost an hour fighting the traffic, they arrived in Nicholson Street, where Berichon jumped out and sprinted off, taking a circuitous route to his home further down the street.

surveillance. Its occupants had endured a tense night, listening to the sounds of the manhunt which had engulfed the area. Abbott, furious at Berichon's behaviour, knew they couldn't stay. And staying together, at least for the moment, was out of the question. At some point in the next few days they would have to split up.

Berichon was morose. He'd not only put them in serious danger of recapture; shooting two cops had turned it into a matter of life or death. But there was still hope. Abbott, ever reliable, had a plan, and Berichon had been included despite his massive indiscretion.

Strategies were planned, essentials packed and by the time the Special Response Squad descended on the cottage on Tuesday, they were already gone.

'These two are Australia's most wanted men,' Detective Senior Sergeant Brian Rix, in charge of the operation, announced to the public two days later. 'We believe at this stage Abbott and Berichon are together. We believe they are at least armed with the nine-millimetre pistol and more than likely armed with revolvers as well. They have been on the run for a long time, and sooner or later we are going to catch up to them. We are telling them now. Give it up.'

For Abbott and Berichon, the odds of escape seemed slim. Roadblocks sprang up around the country in what would develop into arguably the nation's biggest manhunt. The anonymous travel Abbott had enjoyed from 1989 to 1995 was no longer possible. He was now the nation's most prized criminal scalp, and Berichon was wanted on no less than four counts of attempted murder. They got out of Victoria. Fast.

But over the next few days, Melbourne detectives began adding valuable pieces to the puzzle. A thorough search of the cottage had turned up photographs of a young woman in a bikini, a Thai magazine and women's toiletries. Later, the woman in the picture was identified as Ruang Khiankham, an illegal Thai immigrant who now called herself Michelle. She had arrived in Australia in 1995 on a five-day visa and never returned home.

After Berichon met her in Melbourne she stayed at the cottage regularly and, although she spoke little English, the pressure of his situation with Abbott had led to an intense relationship. Infatuated, Berichon had rung her when he arrived in Adelaide with Abbott, where they are believed to have stayed for several days after the shooting. She flew to Adelaide soon after, and the escapees' journey resumed.

Meanwhile, Melbourne detectives had tracked down details of the two vehicles Berichon had bought, and these were widely circulated in the media. On Friday, the LandCruiser was found at Melbourne Airport, but investigators were rightly sceptical about its significance.

calculating sort of person and very intelligent. He has a very high IQ and I don't think he would want to be held back by a liability such as Berichon. So it would not surprise investigators at all if Berichon and Abbott had split up.'

But where were they? Sightings were placing all three at various points around the nation, including, of all places, Old Parliament House in Canberra. A security guard believed he had seen Abbott there on Sunday, April 26. It couldn't have been him, but wanted posters were soon staring down at the nation's politicians, from security posts around new Parliament House.

In Adelaide, Sid Thomas thought he might have something more concrete. Intelligence — correct, as it turned out — had placed Berichon and Michelle in the city in the days after they fled Carlton. On April 28, he received a report that a young man and young Asian woman had been at a backpackers' hostel at Nundroo, between Ceduna and the Western Australian border.

As the evidence began to mount that it was Berichon and Michelle, excitement grew among police on both sides of the border. But when the young man was finally tracked down in Esperance, in Western Australia, it turned out to be another case of mistaken identity.

It wasn't the only one — the distinctive descriptions of a young Caucasian man with a young Asian female led to dozens of couples being placed under surveillance around the nation over the next few days. Surprisingly, each state was still conducting separate police operations, despite the manhunt's national nature. The unofficial police grapevine had been working overtime, and detectives liaised with interstate colleagues as new information came to light. But on an official level, there was nothing. Some wondered if anything had been learned from the mistakes of the past.

Abbott had lived virtually as he pleased from 1989 until 1994, when senior police were finally convinced that a national approach was needed. The flow of intelligence from Probe: Flanders was coordinated through the Australian Bureau of Criminal Intelligence in Canberra after detectives in three states pooled their knowledge and resources. It was no coincidence that he was back behind bars within six months.

Now, there was even a contingency plan for exactly the type of situation the fugitives had created. State police commissioners were signatories to National Major Crime Investigation Management, set up to deal with major situations which crossed state boundaries, but there were no moves to put it into action. If the trail had gone cold after a few weeks, perhaps they may have reconsidered. As it was, there was little time for reflection in the two weeks following the Melbourne shooting.

With Abbott and Berichon flushed out and on the run, each new piece of intelligence brought hope to investigators, who believed it was only a matter of time before they were cornered. Capturing them, however, was another matter entirely and the media were talking up fears of a bloody showdown. Berichon always gone peacefully in the past, the stakes were now much higher. There was no telling what he might do.

Away from the action of the manhunt, the case had taken another unexpected twist. In addition to the hunt for Abbott and Berichon, a secret, parallel police investigation had been under way in Queensland since February. But on April 22, Queensland Premier Rob Borbidge let the cat out of the bag.

The Opposition had mounted a sustained campaign against Prisons Minister Russell Cooper over the Sir David Longland escape and the general state of the prison system. Opposition police spokesman Tom Barton told parliament that the 'inescapable evidence of the Government's failure to effectively manage the prison system was best summed up by four words: Where is Brenden Abbott?'

Frustrated, the Premier replied: 'When you are aware of certain details in regard to that escape and certain matters relating to problems experienced by [Mr Cooper] you will greatly regret that remark.'

The mysterious comment didn't go unnoticed — behind it lay an audacious and violent plot unheard of in Australian criminal history.

The *Courier-Mail*'s chief police reporter, Paula Doneman, who had been sitting on the story for two months, gave a front page explanation of Operation Livid the following Monday:

A drug syndicate plot to launch armed air and ground raids on Queensland jails to free some of the country's most dangerous criminals has been uncovered by police.

The interstate syndicate, made up of four people including notorious armed bandit Brendon Abbott, planned to use stolen helicopters, explosives and high-powered guns to raid the prisons.

The syndicate also is believed to be behind a threat to assassinate Prisons Minister Russell Cooper and an unnamed Sydney businessman.

It is understood the wealthy gang hatched the incredible plan to free the armed robbers in a bid to establish itself at the forefront of organised crime in Australia.

A top-secret Queensland police operation involving up to 60 of the state's elite crimefighters uncovered the plot in February.

The Sir David Longland escape and a breakout from another Queensland prison, Borallon, were alleged to be the first steps in the plan.

The similarities between the two escapes were striking. The Borallon breakout, in February 1998, involved three inmates who had escaped through a toilet window and run to a perimeter fence, where cutting tools had been thrown over by outside accomplices. A mobile phone was believed to have been smuggled into the prison and used to arrange the escape.

After escaping from a residential block, armed robbers Frank Post, Wayne Morrell and Barry Maxworthy ran to a waiting car. Its occupants provided covering fire, engaging in a shoot-out with a female prison officer, who was injured by glass fragments.

But unlike the Sir David Longland escapees, they failed to make it to safety, and were recaptured after crashing the getaway car in a chase.

Judging from the violent and methodical nature of the two escapes, the plot had been well advanced when uncovered by police. Some criminologists claimed it was all the product of loose talk in prison, prompted by the security crackdown in the wake of the Sir David Longland escape. But the police made it clear the threats weren't being taken lightly.

'We take the information very seriously and we have picked some of the best detectives in the state,' Queensland Assistant Police Commissioner Graham Williams told the *Courier-Mail*. 'Nothing is impossible. With the sophistication of organised crime you do not have the option of ignoring the information when we have already seen the murder of a New South Wales politician [John Newman].'

But any thoughts of mass escapes and criminal masterplans were now far from Abbott's mind. He was too busy running.

Chapter 19

Feeling the heat

'Yeah, I'm Brenden Abbott. Suppose this'll make you blokes famous.'

— The fugitive, face down and handcuffed
in a Darwin street, 2 May 1998

After Michelle had arrived in Adelaide, the fugitives headed north by road — next stop, Alice Springs. Abbott's brother, David, still lived in the town, and was now running a tour bus business.

Given the attention his family was now receiving, it seems unlikely that Abbott would have risked a social visit. David's name had already come up in the investigation days after the prison breakout. Media reports said his fingerprints had been found on ammunition outside the prison, and that it was the same as 2000 rounds seized from his home during a raid several years previously. It was also reported that he was nowhere to be found in the days after the escape. But the eldest Abbott brother is understood to have had a good alibi — he was out driving a busload of tourists around the Northern Territory.

On arrival in Alice Springs, Abbott told Berichon and Michelle they would have to split up for a few days. There was

pistol, wigs, a make-up kit and a laptop computer with software used to produce false driver's licences — plus a stash of marijuana, for those quieter, reflective moments on the run.

Abbott's movements in the next few days were difficult to track, but he is believed to have returned to Queensland. Berichon and Michelle, meanwhile, were off on an expensive errand. After arriving in Darwin, they caught a flight to Broome, in north-west Western Australia, and booked into the Roebuck Bay Motel.

Abbott wanted the LandCruiser re-registered under a false name in Western Australia, where it wasn't necessary to produce the vehicle to complete the paperwork. It needed to be squeaky clean in case any curious traffic cop should check its details on the police computer.

Berichon booked into the hotel for three nights, paying $330 cash, and the couple remained in their room virtually the entire time. A 'Do Not Disturb' sign was placed on the door, which remained chained, and they told the cleaner the room was fine, thanks — we just need fresh towels. After the shock of the Melbourne shooting, Berichon seemed to have learned that walking the streets was a dangerous pursuit for a fugitive.

On Wednesday, April 29, they made a phone call and decided not to stay for the third night. After booking out, they headed to the airport for the return journey to Darwin. Later, the media would seize on the call as the turning point in the case. The hotel manager said he believed police had intercepted it. Media reports claimed the call had been made to Abbott, and police had then tracked Berichon to Darwin in the hope that he would rendezvous with Abbott.

It seemed the perfect piece of cloak and dagger in a case already filled with dramatic twists. One newspaper even suggested that the call had been traced via a bug placed inside Abbott's mobile phone. But Jack Lee dismisses the theories out of hand. 'Do you really think we would have let him go on his way when he was wanted for shooting two coppers? The idea is nonsense. At that stage, we believed if we were going to have a problem, it was going to be with Berichon. He was the one I wanted.'

It was actually intelligence — still undisclosed — passed on by the Victorian Special Response Group which led the Western Australian police to the Roebuck Bay Hotel. 'We sent a crew straight around there but they'd already left,' Lee said.

Berichon and Michelle, unaware of their close call, checked into the Luma Luma Holiday Apartments when they arrived back in Darwin and settled into room 608. It was in Knuckey Street in the city's small central business district, perhaps the most easy-going CBD in the nation. But at times over the next few days, it would feel more like a war zone.

Brenden Abbott a free man many times in the past. But this would be a particularly long trip and there were still preparations to be made.

On Wednesday evening, a man calling himself Michael — believed to be Abbott, location unknown — rang a Darwin couple in response to a classified advertisement for a camper trailer. Someone would be around to look at it tomorrow, he promised.

Berichon dropped by the next morning and liked what he saw. 'Michael' rang to confirm the sale on Thursday evening, but wanted the registration transferred — didn't want any trouble with paperwork if he was pulled over, he told them.

The next day, Berichon booked a room at the Top End, a city hotel in Daly Street. Abbott was arriving in town later in the day and the final details for the outback trip would be arranged. Darwin — remote, relaxed and teeming with itinerants — seemed the perfect regrouping point for the fugitives — as long as they remained undetected.

But on Friday, May 1, it all began to fall apart. Intelligence from the Queensland Police indicated that Abbott was about to cross their border into the Northern Territory. The Northern Territory Police, who had had little to do with Abbott in the past, were quickly briefed and placed on full alert. The Territory Response Group dispatched extra officers to border crossings, and roadhouses and remote stations were warned of the danger.

Abbott is believed to have already slipped through, arriving in Darwin and staying at the Top End Hotel that night. For a few hours, at least, he was safe. But Darwin isn't a big city — the Stuart Highway is the only road in and out, and the small airport terminal is easily monitored. The next day, Operation Coconut would shift into top gear.

Had he known, Abbott would have savoured the challenge — he'd faced worse odds. And he'd made plenty of the big city detectives look stupid in the past. How tough could a bunch of country coppers be?

On the morning of May 2, there was still no conclusive evidence to place Abbott in the Northern Territory. But Michelle and Berichon had attracted more attention, with further intelligence from the Victorian Police indicating there was a good chance they were in Darwin.

Detective Senior Sergeant Col Smith and Superintendent George Owen began marshalling their forces, rounding up every available detective and diverting a crew from a homicide inquiry. A check of hotels and motels was quickly organised and photographs of the fugitives were passed out. By mid-afternoon, a trio of officers were questioning the receptionist at the Top End Hotel. She looked at the photograph of Berichon and pointed confidently at the scar on his neck. He'd been wearing a skivvy, but it was still visible, she said.

There wasn't much doubt — wanted posters nationwide specifically mentioned Berichon's habit of trying to hide a distinctive scar by wearing skivvies.

A hasty surveillance operation was set up while the rest of the team was alerted, but events suddenly gathered speed. Senior Constable Mike Dennien, sitting in a nearby park, watched a LandCruiser with trailer pull up at 4.40 pm. 'There was a silver car there and we watched the four-wheel drive back in beside it

Abbott drove a few streets to a laundromat at a shopping precinct in Harriet Place. Pulling a basket from the four-wheel drive, he looked as ordinary as the next man in the street — even the nation's most wanted fugitive could find time to attend to domestic duties. After spending a few minutes inside, he wandered down the street for a quick bite to eat at a takeaway shop. Next came a phone call at a public box across the road, just as two LandCruisers filled with Territory Response Group officers prepared to make their move from either end of the street.

Abbott stopped briefly at his LandCruiser after a trip to the supermarket, then turned to walk back to the laundry, oblivious to the two vehicles bearing down on him. A few metres away, two men enjoying a beer on the balcony of Parkhaven Lodge watched with bemusement as the drama unfolded.

'We looked around and there were police in the park with their scopes lined up at us,' Mark Garner later told the *NT News*. 'Then I saw the guy walk out. He wasn't looking around or anything. The police pointed their guns and yelled "get down on the ground" at him. He got on his knees and they pushed him down. He looked stunned.'

Last time, in Queensland, Abbott had almost expected it. But Darwin? It was the last place on earth he expected to get caught, he later said. There was no attempt to feign surprise or lie about his identity, and no move to reach for the standard bum bag with loaded pistol.

Face down and handcuffed amid a sea of flak jackets and high-powered police weapons, he was the picture of defeat. But there was an image to be maintained. He tried for a line to fit the occasion. 'Yeah, I'm Brenden Abbott. Suppose this'll make you blokes famous,' he offered grudgingly.

Col Smith had been in the background, awaiting the result nervously. 'I went forward to see if it was Abbott. I was relieved. I was worried we might have ruined some tourist's day,' he said.

After the 'traveller's kit' was uncovered in the LandCruiser, Sergeant Scott Pollock was given the task of driving it back to police headquarters — on the outskirts of the city — with Mike Dennien following behind.

'About halfway along Tiger Brennan Drive, I came across Scott waving cars down with a torch. The tyre had blown out. We wanted to add a charge of attempted murder,' Dennien commented wryly.

fingerprints.

'He was very belligerent and unhappy, but he didn't swear or curse and he was reasonably well spoken,' Acting Commander Gary Manison later told the *NT News*. 'For purposes of identification we asked for his fingerprints — when he refused we told him we would take them by force if we had to. He said "come on, have a go" and got upset and lashed out. I think he was in a state of shock.'

But by the next day, Abbott had calmed down, beginning to revel in the excitement and attention his recapture had caused. There had always between a grudging respect between Abbott and many of his pursuers, but his notoriety had added a new dimension — the criminal celebrity.

Police officers — detectives, in particular — are suckers for career mementos. On their office walls, veterans hang plaques bearing CIB squad insignias, newspaper articles from big cases and commendations from on-the-job incidents. Abbott's contribution would be unique — signed wanted posters. 'Could've at least let me finish my laundry. BJ Abbott,' one read.

When Jack Lee arrived from Perth a few days later, Abbott scrawled a message to his old foes: 'To the Perth Armed Robbery Squad: Be home soon. BJ Abbott.'

'He pulled the bloody pen apart after he signed it,' Lee said, incredulous. Abbott's mind was back on the job. As early as Sunday, he dictated a press release over the phone to solicitor Chris Nyst in Queensland. In typically ocker fashion, Abbott expressed surprise at the claims of assassination plans and breakout plots.

'I don't know whether the police put that story out just to make me look bad, or whether it was dreamt up by some lunatic, but I can tell you it's just not true,' he told Nyst. 'I've never thought about killing Cooper or anyone else . . . That sort of thing is just not my go. I don't know whether it's a political move or what . . . I just don't understand what the motive is.'

And he was 'flabbergasted' by the reports of his involvement in a mass breakout plot. 'I don't know where they get these things from. Whoever came up with that is just dreaming . . . it's absurd. The only bloke I've ever planned to spring out of jail is Brenden Abbott.'

Watching the news in the city apartment on Saturday night, Brendan Berichon would have despaired at his situation. His

Detectives sat in restaurants, on park benches and in hotels.

They watched people relieve themselves in flower boxes, got abused by drunks, attracted a nutter who kept pointing at passing cars for them, and watched lonely people wander back and forth in the night.

But Berichon, caught like a rabbit in a spotlight, didn't dare move from his room.

On Sunday, police announced a $50 000 reward and warned

that Berichon was believed to be armed with two semi-automatic weapons. Two comprehensive checks on all accommodation in the city had turned up nothing. A third was ordered, and this time registration cards were physically checked for all guests who had paid cash, arrived on April 29, or hadn't left their rooms.

The net was closing rapidly. But for once, it was Abbott's cleverness, rather than his own stupidity, which finally brought Berichon undone.

Late on Monday morning, a Bureau of Criminal Intelligence officer checking through items seized from Abbott began examining his brown leather wallet. There appeared to be something scratched into its exterior, and he placed it under a light in the fingerprint bureau for closer examination. It looked like a local phone number, which was easily checked on a reverse phone directory — it was listed to the Luma Luma Apartments.

It had already been checked three times, but Sergeant Les Chapman and Senior Constable Debbie Harris were dispatched to check through the registration cards. The receptionist was sorting through them when Chapman noticed her flick past one marked 'Paid Cash.' The guy hadn't wanted a receipt, she said, but she was sure it wasn't Berichon.

Jason Parker, in room 608. But Jason seemed to have had some trouble with his name, originally writing an 'F' instead of 'J'. And the address was Miller Street, Kirwan, a suburb in Berichon's home town of Townsville.

Given the phone number on Abbott's wallet, it sounded promising. They pressed the receptionist for more details. She finally agreed that yes, the woman could have been Asian and the 'dorky-looking' guy in a baseball cap could have been Berichon.

area. They had just been briefed at police headquarters at Berrimah, and were heading into the business district expecting an interview with a Territory Response Group officer. There was a sudden change of plans. The officer had suddenly become 'unavailable', and they were asked to wait in a hotel car park.

But *NT News* chief of staff Greg Thomson, on a day off, saw a Territory Response Group vehicle travelling at a great rate of knots, and it wasn't long before cameras were trained on the apartments from every angle. The surrounding streets were virtually deserted, with only a few 'couples' doing their best to look casual and inconspicuous.

But while Berichon was now believed to be contained in the hotel, he was still armed, several floors up and had access to a balcony. He'd been out a few times, looking around nervously at the eerily quiet street. The phone call from the negotiator came as no surprise.

There were no sudden explosions of rage or volleys of gunshots. Although desperate, Berichon wasn't suicidal and he quickly indicated his desire to surrender. Michelle left the room first, but there was a hitch — Berichon, still infatuated, wanted to bring some pictures of her with him.

No, we'd prefer it if you didn't have anything in your hands, the negotiator explained.

A few minutes later, Michelle emerged from the apartment car park, hunched down in the back seat of a police car. Berichon followed, handcuffed and head bowed in the back of a cage car, sporting a mane of bleached hair which gave him a markedly different appearance to his mugshot.

It was over. In less than 48 hours, the nation's two most wanted men had been arrested without a shot being fired. A short time later, Northern Territory Police Commissioner Brian Bates savoured his officers' success in front of the cameras. 'It has been simply an outstanding effort by the men and women of the Northern Territory police force. Over the past six days, the efforts of the Crime Command — and I particularly mention the Bureau of Criminal Intelligence, the Territory Response Group, and the men and women of the uniform section — have been magnificent,' he said.

'I also wish to thank the members of the Northern Territory public for their patience and understanding over the last three days. There has been considerable disruption to their movement and there has been a need for obvious police activity in and around Darwin.'

While careful to mention the vital contributions of Queensland and Victorian police, the commissioner saved the ultimate compliment for his own officers. 'The Northern Territory public, in my view, has an extremely high regard for their police force. We might not be the biggest, but I believe you will agree with me that with the capture of Abbott and Berichon, we have shown the rest of Australia we are the best.'

The rest of the nation seemed to agree. Congratulatory phone calls and faxes flooded in from the police and public.

Queensland Police Minister Russell Cooper was 'a very happy man', and vowed Abbott would never escape from prison again. 'We have a nice new comfortable cell for him at the

Chapter 20

Case closed?

'He's prepared to cop what's coming to him.'
— Solicitor Chris Nyst, outside Brisbane
Magistrates Court, 29 June 1998

At 9.18 the next morning, Brendan Berichon made his public debut, stepping from the cells into the dock of Darwin Magistrates Court. He glanced nervously around the courtroom — packed with hungover detectives from four states, plus local and national media — and then stared ahead, sullen.

The Victorians had been given first shot at him, and the prosecutor asked Magistrate Greg Cavanagh for an adjournment until the next morning. Domestic airlines had expressed some discomfort at the idea of carrying Berichon, and the detectives needed time to make transport arrangements. Berichon had no objection.

'I suppose it's academic, but is there an application for bail?' the magistrate asked. Berichon allowed himself a wry smile. If only. He was led back to the cells, barefoot and still in the shirt and shorts he'd been wearing when arrested.

told him, and remanded Abbott to be held in custody at Berriman Jail until transport to Brisbane could be arranged.

On May 6, accompanied by three Victorian detectives, Brendan Berichon was extradited to Melbourne after the airline was convinced he wouldn't be a problem.

At the time of writing, he had pleaded guilty to charges of assaulting police and kidnapping over the events in Melbourne, but pleaded not guilty to the two counts of attempted murder, saying his actions were reckless, not intentional.

Like many before him, Berichon lived to regret ever meeting Brenden Abbott — his sheet-metal apprenticeship may not have paid much, but its longer-term prospects must now seem a lot better than his career in crime.

In Perth, Glenn Abbott remains in Casuarina Prison, after being sentenced to eight years without parole for the shooting of Senior Constable Lee Watson. At the time of writing, he was appealing the conviction.

In sentencing submissions, his lawyer, Richard Bayly, noted

that Abbott had been held in the prison's special handling unit for a total of 14 months while his brother was on the run — just in case. After the prison stabbing, he served another four months in solitary, which was taken into account when he finally pleaded guilty late in 1998.

Another three years were added to his sentence, this time with eligibility for parole, but it will be at least 2005 before he has a realistic chance of being released.

For him, there were few regrets. After the heady days of living covertly and working with his fugitive brother, it hadn't turned out quite how he had hoped. But the brothers remain loyal, and Glenn enjoys the status his role in Brenden's career has brought him.

And while he never earned the same headlines, and would be forever known as 'Brenden Abbott's brother', he knew the police would always now take him a lot more seriously. They know that while Brenden may be dangerous, Glenn remains unpredictable — which he had proved was a far more frightening prospect.

Once again, Brenden Abbott sits in a small cell in the high-security section of a maximum security prison. The same day Berichon returned to Melbourne, he was flown by a government-owned jet back to Brisbane. A helicopter and car ride later, he was in the magistrates court being charged with escaping legal custody and four counts of preventing arrest by attempting to fire a weapon.

The repercussions of the escape on the state's prison system and political scene were far-reaching. Heads rolled and there was a wide-scale shake-up of the system's running and structure.

reflect on the mayhem a single man managed to cause across the nation in just over a decade.

Elmer Fudd, Hiker, Braille, Jilt, Flanders, Passion, Razor, Korn, Livid, Coconut — there was a name for every occasion, and at one time or another, virtually every state and federal law enforcement agency had pursued him. There had been victories and losses along the way, as well as Hollywood-style crimes and touches of humour. For the public, it was the perfect tale of crime — there was an Abbott and Costello, a Thelma and Louise, and comedy and road trips to match. But at what cost?

Estimates of Abbott's total haul from armed robberies range from $3 million to $5 million, but it is a mere drop in the ocean compared to what he has cost Australian taxpayers since 1986.

The cost to police to investigate, capture and recapture Abbott was enormous. On top of hundreds of officers who pursued him full-time at one time or another, he generated overtime which ran into hundreds of thousands of hours.

Through Legal Aid, lengthy trials, appeals and a 'never plead guilty' attitude, he compiled another figure in the inestimable millions. In addition, there were the regular and expensive high-security operations which surrounded every appearance Abbott made in court.

And the human cost — to bank staff and their families, and the many young men he drew down a dangerous path — can never be measured in dollars.

On 4 September 1998, Brenden Abbott was rather belatedly declared a serious violent offender in the Brisbane District Court and sentenced to a further six years over the charges related to his escape.

Added to the time he already owed Queensland and Western Australian prisons, he would have to serve at least a further 32 years in jail — and he is yet to face other charges in Western Australia and South Australia which range from armed robbery to escaping legal custody.

It is virtually a life sentence, but Abbott has shown before that he is a patient man. In his Woodford cell, he watches. And waits.

Permissions

The author and publisher are grateful to the following for their co-operation in making this book possible:

Permission to quote from Queensland court transcripts involving Brenden James Abbott was kindly granted by the Department of Justice and Attorney-General. The copyright of this material belongs to the State of Queensland and the reproduced material is not an official copy.

Permission to quote from Western Australia court transcripts involving Brenden James Abbott and Glenn Norman Abbott was kindly granted by the West Australian Attorney General. The copyright of this material belongs to the State of Western Australia and the reproduced material is not an official copy.

Permission to quote excerpts from 'The Making of An Anti-Hero' by Frank Robson was kindly granted by *Good Weekend*.

ISBN 0 7322 6770 6

The Jaidyn Leskie Murder

BY MICHAEL GLEESON

On New Year's Day in 1998, the body of an infant child was discovered in Blue Rock Dam near the town of Moe in eastern Victoria. Although the body had been submerged for some time, the cold water in the dam had prevented rapid decomposition. To Detective Senior Sergeant Rowland Legg of Victoria's homicide squad, the child's face was instantly recognisable. It was a face that had been etched into Australia's national consciousness, and conscience, since a little boy had disappeared in bizarre circumstances six months earlier. It was the face of Jaidyn Raymond Leskie.

The discovery of Jaidyn's battered body brought to a close one of the biggest searches for a missing person in Australia's history. However, it did little to answer the myriad questions surrounding the murder. What happened on the night of Jaidyn's disappearance? What was the relevance of a pig's head, found on the front lawn of the house from which he allegedly vanished? How could a society such as ours have allowed this heinous crime to happen? And, most importantly, who killed Jaidyn, and why?

ISBN 0 7322 6464 2

Mercy: In Pursuit of the Truth about the Death of Yvonne Gilford

BY MICK O'DONNELL

For many months during the imprisonment of British nurses Deborah Parry and Lucille McLauchlan, Australian journalist Mick O'Donnell was the only point of contact between the women and the man who held their lives in his hand. Accused of murdering their Australian colleague, Yvonne Gilford, in a Saudi Arabian hospital in December 1996, the two women were facing death by the sword, unless the brother of the victim granted mercy.

This is Mick O'Donnell's account of the attempt to create dialogue between the accused women fearing for their lives and the man who wanted justice for his dead sister. While all other Western journalists were refused admission to the country to cover the case, the Saudi authorities allowed O'Donnell to take a television team into the Kingdom to cover the story. This exclusive access gave him contact with all the players in the case: the families of the women and the dead nurse, the lawyers for both sides, the police and other hospital staff.

ISBN 0 7322 5981 9

Never to be Released: Volume 2

BY PAUL B. KIDD

Murderers, rapists, psychopaths...

In many parts of the world, these sorts of criminals can expect retribution by firing squad, lethal injection, the noose or, more macabrely, the electric chair. In Australia, our courts sentence them to a life of incarceration — 'never to be released'.

This recommendation is usually reserved solely for the worst of the worst: the child killers, those who rape and murder in pairs and packs, the serial killers, the mass murderers. But now that list includes a man who attempted to murder a tourist, another who set a little boy alight, and a heroin dealer.

In this frank and compelling book, Paul B. Kidd, a respected authority on this gruesome rollcall of humanity, looks at recent cases that have resulted in the handing down of a 'never to be released' recommendation or its equivalent, the threads that link Australia's serial killers, and the arguments for and against capital punishment.

All the horrific crimes in this book actually happened. Fortunately, all their perpetrators are where they belong — behind bars — 'never to be released'.